Honourable Friends

By the same author

All Good Men (1987)

Honourable Friends

Janet Daley

Weidenfeld and Nicolson
London

For Emma and Melissa
who have endured this enterprise
with such patience.

First published in Great Britain in 1989 by
George Weidenfeld and Nicolson Limited
91 Clapham High Street, London SW4 7TA

British Library Cataloguing-in-Publication Data

Daley, Janet
Honourable friends.
I. Title
823'.914 [F]

ISBN 0–297–79614–3

Photoset and printed in Great Britain by
Redwood Burn Limited, Trowbridge, Wiltshire

‘Evil is always commonplace.’

This story is set in either a recent imaginary past or a possible near future. References to real persons by name or by office are used solely to create a credible setting for fictitious events and characters.

J.D.

Part One

'BUT YOU'RE NOT committing yourself to doing anything,' Priscilla protested.

'It isn't that,' Beth muttered.

'What is it then?'

'He just thinks it's rather fascist.'

'What?' The shock in Priscilla's voice was so genuine that the remark seemed ludicrous even to Beth. Embarrassment made her more defensive. 'He dislikes all this property-owning obsession,' she persevered.

'But you do own your house, don't you, Beth.' Priscilla was taking on the tone one would use with an overtired child. 'All that the Neighbourhood Watch scheme is doing is getting people to keep an eye on each other's homes for everyone's protection.'

'Vigilante-ism, Jim calls it,' Beth retorted.

'Oh, for God's sake, it's only what old-fashioned neighbours have always done for each other. When I was a child my father caught somebody breaking into the garage next door and chased him half way down the road. It's only natural not to stand by when you see someone's home being broken into.'

'I'm not saying you should stand by and watch somebody

being burgled,' Beth replied hurriedly. Then falling back on the authority of her husband, 'Jim just doesn't like the bourgeois homeowner thing – and getting chatty with the police.'

'What's wrong with the police?' Priscilla was running out of patience. 'You'd be glad enough to have them around if you were attacked.'

'Oh, for heaven's sake, it's not that.'

'I'm afraid I'm not following this at all, Beth.' Priscilla was beginning to sound really annoyed. Trapped between her husband's intransigence and Priscilla's objections, Beth became conciliatory. 'Look, I'll talk to him again about it tonight, all right?'

'Yes, all right,' Priscilla said, softening her voice.

'You're going to Rachel's tomorrow night, aren't you?' Beth continued, taking the conversation out of this contentious arena.

'Mmm,' Priscilla murmured, running her pencil down the list of people she had still to contact about Neighbourhood Watch.

'Are Helen and Max going?' Beth carried on, wanting to continue into amiability.

'Don't think so,' Priscilla said. 'He's still in Germany.' *You and Jim were invited*, she thought, *because Helen and Max couldn't come.*

'Oh, that's a shame. Jim likes them.'

'I've got to ring off, Beth. Got some more people to phone before I go in to the gallery.' Priscilla tried not to sound abrupt but Beth responded as though she had been put down. 'Oh, are you going in today? You don't usually work on Fridays, do you?' Her voice was accusatory.

'Not usually, but we're getting ready to hang a new show.'

'Why should you have to be there for that?' The earlier argument made her cattiness about Priscilla's job more unguarded.

'Everyone comes in to help when we're hanging,' Priscilla replied. Beth always seemed to assume that she was flaunting the importance of her job as an art gallery publicist. She acknowledged Priscilla's self-deprecating answer with an indeterminate noise.

'Anyway, we'll see you tomorrow night and Jim can tell us all about his objections to Neighbourhood Watch.' Beth laughed good-naturedly. 'Okay,' she said. 'See you then.'

Priscilla put the telephone down as Julian arrived at the bottom of the stairs in their basement kitchen. He looked tired even after a long lie-in, still exhausted from his two-day trip to New York.

'You're not going in, are you?' she asked, taking in the fact that he was obviously dressed for the office. He nodded as he went to pour himself some coffee.

'Do you really have to?' she asked, knowing that in his fatigue, this perseverance risked provoking him. He made an affirmative noise, apparently without irritation. Carrying his mug of coffee to the refectory table, he sat down. 'Won't be for long. Just have to ring New York and make sure the stuff has been faxed to Brussels.'

'Do you want anything to eat?'

He thought for a moment, sipping his coffee. Even a decision about breakfast was slow in coming. 'Scrambled eggs,' he said finally. She stood up from the stool on which she had been sitting to make her telephone calls, and removed two eggs from their wooden rack on the work surface. As she whisked them in the bowl, she said, 'Jim and Beth won't join Neighbourhood Watch.'

He turned in surprise, 'Why the hell not?'

'He seems to think it's too middle class,' she said archly.

'He is bloody middle class.'

Priscilla smiled over the frying pan. 'He doesn't like admitting it to himself.'

'He makes twenty-five thousand a year, for Christ's sake,' Julian said, his mental agility revived by the outrage.

'Still the working class hero,' Priscilla said, sliding the eggs on to a plate.

'He was never working class,' Julian protested as she set the eggs down in front of him. 'Just because he's from Sheffield doesn't make him working class. His father owned a shop. Beth told me at a party when she was pissed. His parents were the height of provincial respectability apparently.'

'Well,' Priscilla said, sitting down next to him. 'Neighbourhood Watch is altogether too bourgeois for his radical conscience.'

Julian shook his head as he speared a mound of egg with his fork. 'He ought to bloody well grow up.'

Priscilla glanced up at the clock on the wall. It was nearly half-past eleven. Krista would be going to collect Emily from playgroup. She would have to get herself organized to leave or she would be caught up in Emily's lunch time routine. It was best to be out of the house before they returned.

'You'll be home early, then?' she asked Julian.

'Should be,' he said, polishing off the last of his egg. His voice was strengthened by the nourishment and she knew that this non-committal answer meant that he would probably decide to spend the rest of the day at the office.

'Try to be,' she said gently. He nodded vaguely, accepting her concern with blithe inattention.

'I'll be back around five,' she said, gathering up her keys and umbrella. He glanced obligingly over his coffee mug, his eyes brighter and less fogged. She decided that perhaps he would be able to cope with a day at the office after all.

* * *

The rain had stopped by the time she reached the gallery. She shook her umbrella vigorously and pressed the concealed doorbell. Simon's head appeared at the top of the stairs that led up from the basement as the buzzer sounded unlocking the glass door. Priscilla stepped onto the polished floorboards gingerly and immediately slipped out of her wet shoes. Carrying her umbrella and shoes to the reception desk, she heard Simon's voice call from downstairs. 'We're down here, love.'

The larger paintings were all hung but the smaller ones and the lithographs still lay propped against the white walls. They always repainted the walls before each new show. Set against these huge abstract canvases with their mass of primary colours, the whiteness looked starkly dazzling. The paintings seemed to float away from the walls, great oceans of colour taking on a presence quite disproportionate to their artistic substance. Tricked by the retina, the mind seemed to respond to this overload of sensation with mystical shock. Priscilla stepped down the open tread staircase in her stockinged feet hearing voices floating up from the further corner of the basement storeroom. 'Can't put it in with *those*,' Simon was saying emphatically. 'The recent ones are so much better. This will look thin and tatty.'

A lower murmur responded in apparent agreement. Priscilla made her way through the racks of paintings toward the voices. Simon was standing over a small canvas, his narrow face wrinkled in critical appraisal. Sitting on a stool next to him, Bertie looked morose and anxious. 'But he says he wants it to go in, Simon. He'll be *upset*.'

Simon shook his head and muttered, 'Oh, shit. We'll put it at the back over the desk. Thank God it's small.'

Priscilla stood next to Simon and gazed down at the picture. Dating from five years before, its colours were much paler, its geometry more apparent than the thunderous, uninhibited paintings upstairs. She said, 'He's terribly sentimental about that one. He says that it represented a crucial transition for him when he began to leave constructivism behind.'

'Oh, God,' Simon said.

'He obviously thinks it has a historical importance in his development,' Bertie said loyally.

'Well,' Simon sighed, 'in it will have to go.'

Bertie stood up and picked up the painting, 'Is this all to go upstairs?'

Simon nodded. As Bertie moved past them toward the staircase, he said to Simon in tones of agonized confidentiality, 'Tell Priscilla the bad news.'

She looked at Simon expectantly. Simon winced at her and said, 'I think we'd better have a drink first.'

Priscilla followed Simon's leather trousers up the narrow stairs. By the time she reached the top, Bertie had already disappeared into the back office and was busying himself with the gin and tonic.

'You look quite fetching in bare feet, darling.' Simon smiled at her.

'Didn't want to leave wet footprints,' she said as they sat down on the sofa in the office.

'Would be foul weather, wouldn't it?' Bertie muttered.

'There are two more pictures being delivered today. It's going to be hell getting them in here from the van if it's pouring with rain.'

'What's the bad news, then?'. She turned to Simon.

Simon shut his eyes for tragic emphasis and whispered, 'Macmasters has decided to sell.'

Priscilla looked satisfactorily shocked. 'The whole collection?' she asked, appalled.

Simon nodded and threw his eyes heavenward. 'It's too awful,' Bertie said miserably.

'Does Harold know yet?'

Bertie shook his head hurriedly. 'And he mustn't. Not before the opening, anyway.'

'And,' Simon said, 'no one else must know either until this show is over. Otherwise we will not shift a single picture at an acceptable price.'

'But why is he doing it?' Priscilla asked.

Bertie shrugged. 'He's just got tired of them, he says.' His voice became peevish. 'If the wretched man had got tired of them one at a time, we could have bought them back as they came up but we can't possibly take on the whole lot at once.'

'How will he do it? Put them up at Sotheby's?' Priscilla said.

'I expect so. And they're much too big for private buyers. So the bottom will fall right out of Harold's prices,' Simon groaned.

'He needn't dump the whole lot of them on the market at once, surely,' Priscilla argued.

'No, he needn't,' Bertie agreed. 'But he will. Because that's what he wants to do and people that rich do what they want to do when they want to do it.'

'My God,' Priscilla said quietly.

'Quite,' Simon said, finishing the last of his gin.

'There's only one remote hope,' Bertie said, refilling his glass.

'Bertie's had a brilliant idea,' Simon said cattily, 'which hasn't a hope in hell of coming off.'

Bertie hunched forward conspiratorially. 'We just might be able to persuade Macmasters to offer them to the nation. He's not all that interested in the money so making a gift of them wouldn't worry him and the collection could be called the Macmasters Collection so he'd get some immortality in the process. And it would be very good for Harold.'

'To be housed at the Tate?' she asked.

'Not possible,' Simon put in. 'If the whole collection is to be housed together which is the only thing Macmasters would be interested in, they'd have to go somewhere else. The Tate hasn't the room.'

'That,' Priscilla said slowly, 'is a very large problem.'

'Yes, it is,' Bertie conceded.

'If there were the will to do it from the right quarters,' she rallied, 'I'm sure somewhere could be found to house them. Macmasters might even be prepared to help with the cost of providing a place for them if the country took them.'

Bertie brightened. 'That's absolutely right. I'm sure he would.'

'What it would need,' Simon said, losing his reluctance to entertain the idea, 'is a sympathetic government source to make the right noises so that we could get Macmasters interested. Then we could handle the negotiations.'

'It would have to be done through the Arts Council, wouldn't it?' she asked.

'No, not unless they were taking it for their own collection. The galleries purchase and accept gifts independently.'

'It's all terribly complicated,' Bertie admitted. 'So many people to nobble. If the Tate or the V. & A. said that, in theory, they would like them but had no place to house them, then we could start looking for another location as a kind of annexe to the main gallery.'

Simon was shaking his head hopelessly. 'It's all much too slow. By the time you'd lobbied enough of the Museum trustees, Macmasters would have lost patience and sold up.'

Priscilla laid her empty glass on the floor at her feet. 'But what if the country just took them as an independent collection like the Wallace Collection, on the understanding that Macmasters would set up some sort of trust to help with the housing of them?'

Simon and Bertie both fell silent, digesting this possibility.

'It would certainly be a quicker route,' Simon granted.

'And it circumvents the big museums,' Bertie said hopefully.

'Who would we have to talk to?' Priscilla asked.

Simon's face brightened and he said with slow emphasis, 'I can tell you one thing that could be very useful. The Junior Environment Minister, Thurston, is an admirer of Harold's. He bought a couple of the earlier paintings. His department would be involved in the housing arrangements because the old Public Buildings and Works responsibilities have been taken over by Environment. We've invited him to the opening. Let's pray that he comes.'

'What's he like?' Priscilla asked.

'Very smooth and ambitious,' Bertie said rather bitchily.

'I believe,' Simon smirked, 'that he's quite a man with the ladies.' He turned to Priscilla. 'So we'll have to count on you, dear.'

Priscilla smiled. 'I'll see what I can do.'

The front doorbell rang. Bertie hopped out of his chair and looked round the office door.

'It's the van,' he said.

They all leapt up and walked through to the front of the gallery. Priscilla pressed the buzzer behind the reception desk to release the lock on the door and Simon unrolled a sheet of felt on the floor so that the large paintings could be lifted in without damaging their corners.

'Thank God, the rain's stopped,' Bertie sighed as he bustled out the door to greet the van.

* * *

'We're not going to have an evening's diatribe from Jim, are we?' Julian was brushing his jacket with fussy self-concern.

'Not unless something sets him off,' Priscilla said.

'It doesn't take much.' Julian was never overly enthusiastic about neighbourhood dinner parties but there was a prevailing irritability as well brought on by pressure of work. Fortunately, Peter and Rachel Jupp's dinners were sufficiently relaxed not to add to the strain but she would have to watch carefully for the cues that he was ready to leave. Emily and Jaimie were watching television in their pyjamas when Priscilla came downstairs and Krista made reminders about bedtime as they received their goodbye kisses.

It was less than a mile to Rachel's and so finding a parking place took nearly as long as the drive. Most of the large homes on this Highgate road had been converted into flats and the two or three cars attached to every house were now lined up in relentlessly closed ranks along the kerb. As they walked back around the corner from where they had parked, they coincided with Jim and Beth at the Jupps' front door.

'Had to park around the block,' Julian muttered, explaining the surprising direction from which they were arriving. Jim grunted. 'You can never park along here.'

Beth smiled heartily. 'Fortunately, we live close enough to walk.' It occurred to Julian depressingly that this fact would liberate Jim to drink as much as he liked tonight. Peter opened the door then, ushering them with attentive cordiality into the startling expanse which opened out behind the Victorian porch. Being an architect, Peter preferred larger, more adventurous domestic spaces to conventional rooms and had, in the pursuit of what he called 'vertical vistas', scooped out the innards of their villa leaving a cavernous, barn-like shell, with the remains of the first floor cantilevered around the perimeter as a kind of mezzanine. An open spiral staircase led to the balconied bedrooms on this abbreviated floor, replacing the mahogany bannisters which had guided the way so benignly to nineteenth-century beds. Peter had devoted a good deal of attention to the removal of visual obstruction and there was now a clear view of the roof rafters from the quarry tiled ground floor, a series of flying buttresses projecting out to support what had been the attic. Some of what was gained in unfettered panorama had, however, been lost in privacy and soundproofing. The Jupps' sixteen-year-old son could be heard practising electronic music on his synthesizer in some unidentifiable upstairs location.

Rachel waved from the kitchen area which consisted of a space demarcated by a peninsula of engineering brick and exposed plumbing at the rear of the huge ground floor. She walked through to join them as they sat down on the two large sofas which faced each other across a coffee table of glass and black steel. Peter poured drinks busily while Rachel greeted them all with her usual exuberance. Jim dropped down heavily on to the sofa next to Julian, stretching his legs out in front of him. Nestling his gin and tonic in the palm of his hand, Jim turned laconically. 'How's the world of commerce?' he asked, labouring the words with mild sarcasm.

'Thriving,' Julian replied. He revolved his own glass to redistribute the ice and countered, 'How's the world of local bureaucracy?' Jim was chief planning officer for the borough which permitted him a degree of condescension toward those 'in trade', this peculiarly aristocratic snobbery lying quite comfortably unexamined alongside his socialism. Rachel and Priscilla were talking animatedly about the exhibition which was due to open at Priscilla's gallery. Rachel, who had trained at art school as a painter, took a great interest in all the art world gossip which Priscilla brought back from her job. On the far end of the sofa, Beth sat sullenly listening. Priscilla was relating an anecdote about one of the art critics who came in frequently to be lunched by Bertie.

'I don't know how you cope with all those pseuds,' Beth blurted during a pause. Priscilla subsided unsurprised. 'It has its moments,' she said unoffended. Beth, provoked further by Priscilla's serenity, elaborated. 'I couldn't work with people if I thought they were phoney or dishonest.'

Rachel stood up from where she had perched on the arm of a sofa and said brightly, 'Let's have some food.' They arranged themselves, under her supervision, around the dining table which, also being in glass and black steel, looked like a parent of the coffee table. Over the soup, Peter related his plans for the further stages of the house whose conversion was not yet complete. There was apparently to be a rear extension with a roof garden which would be reached by an outside staircase.

As Rachel served the main course of veal escalopes, Jim looked across the table at Julian and smirked. 'What's this I hear about you organizing the local militia?' he asked, helping himself to a spoonful of courgettes. Caught by surprise, Julian looked blank but Priscilla, on Jim's right, understood immediately.

'What on earth do you find objectionable about neighbours

keeping an eye on each other's houses?' she asked innocently. Jim smiled. 'Put like that,' he said with exaggerated patience, 'it sounds perfectly innocuous.'

'How else could it be put?' Rachel asked, joining in with characteristic energy. Jim's smile became broader. He had obviously anticipated this argument with some relish. 'Joining in the great middle class paranoia about crime,' he proclaimed, 'is less to the point than tackling its root causes.' Beth, sitting opposite, smiled smugly. This pronouncement had, Priscilla suspected, been rehearsed for her benefit earlier and Beth was waiting now with confident pride for its effect. From his end of the table, Peter asked mildly, 'And how are we to do that?'

Jim sensed the danger in this deceptively naive question and looked down at his veal as he replied, 'Well obviously, the solution can only be political.'

'Aah,' Peter said with gentle irony. Julian, to whom the original provocation had been directed, felt obliged to defend his own position. 'So crime is all part of the class war, is it?'

'Everything,' Rachel put in, 'is part of the class war for Jim.'

Jim looked up eagerly, 'Oh, yes,' he said, 'your lot have defined the class war out of existence, haven't you?'

'Our lot,' Rachel retorted, 'have recognized that it's a thing of the past.'

'Can't go on living in the thirties forever, Jim,' Peter scolded benignly. Beth, sensing an ambush for her husband, pulled Rachel into a friendly layby. 'How are you getting on with the party? You're treasurer now, aren't you?' she asked with oblique respect. Rachel nodded. 'We're recruiting like mad for the next local elections.' She looked up at Beth and grinned. 'Don't suppose you want to sign up?'

Jim snorted. 'They're nowhere, you know. All this balance of power crap. When it comes down to it, people will vote for a party not a miscellaneous bunch of opportunists. They want to see clear-cut policies.'

'We have got policies,' Rachel retorted. 'Just because they're not extreme, it doesn't mean they're not clear-cut.'

'Hear, hear,' Priscilla murmured, impressed by the astuteness of Rachel's debating point. Jim made an incensed noise through a mouthful of rice. 'How clear-cut can their policies be?' he expostulated after swallowing. 'They say themselves that they'd be willing to bend them in order to form a government with anybody.'

'That,' Peter said, his voice heavy with untiring equanimity, 'is simply an attempt to be reasonable and achieve compromise.'

'Moderation,' Julian said, 'has to be the only way. Politics has to grow up.'

'Bloody hell,' Jim exploded. 'That's not politics, it's power broking. Apparently,' he went on furiously, 'in the last by-election, the buggers were actually sending out different campaign literature to Labour and Tory supporters.'

'I don't see what's wrong with that,' Priscilla said but her voice sounded vaguely doubtful. Jim sneered, 'Could've been nasty if they'd got into the wrong envelopes.'

'The point is,' Peter lectured kindly, 'we have to achieve some sort of consensus if the country isn't to swing back and forth like a pendulum. We have to take the polarity out of politics.'

'Take the politics out of politics,' Jim grunted.

'But Jim,' Rachel turned to him with appealing fervour, 'it isn't a football match or a war. Politics has to be about letting ordinary people live decently. Most people don't want anything to do with ideology.'

'That's only because,' Jim replied, 'they don't understand how it relates to their lives.'

'God knows,' Julian said wryly, 'your lot have tried hard enough to teach them.'

Rachel stood up to clear the plates and Peter retired to organize the pudding course. With their preoccupied absence, the argument's passion subsided. Beth, hoping to shunt the conversation off of Jim's favourite track, looked across at Priscilla. 'What's this new exhibition going to be like, then?' she asked, with the truculent edge which her tone always carried when enquiring about what she described privately as Priscilla's glamour job.

'He's a colour field painter,' Priscilla answered.

'He paints fields?' Jim asked facetiously.

'Fields of colour,' Priscilla said, 'not real fields.'

'Abstracts, you mean,' Beth said, as if Priscilla had been deliberately mystifying.

'Yes,' Priscilla agreed, 'large abstract paintings.'

'Mmm,' Beth murmured dubiously.

'I quite like them,' Priscilla said staunchly. 'The latest ones he's done are very striking.'

'Would you want to live with them, though?' Jim asked sceptically.

'Live with whom?' Rachel asked, rejoining the table.

'Not whom, what,' Julian said helpfully.

'Live with Harold Lewis's paintings,' Priscilla explained.

'Oh,' Rachel said. 'I wouldn't mind. If I had a big enough space to hang them. They need scale. They're all about space, really.' Jim snorted slightly. Rachel looked at him with amiable frankness. 'Do you think that's a terribly pretentious remark?' Embarrassed by her candour, he smirked and said, 'I could never really see abstract paintings as being *about* anything.'

'They're about what they are – colour and space,' Peter said in his benevolent, authoritative voice. Jim made a noise which implied that he was unconvinced.

'I didn't like that sort of thing much when I first started at the gallery,' Priscilla ventured accommodatingly, 'but they've grown on me. I think I see the point of them now.'

'I suppose,' Jim muttered, 'that's what it's all about – seeing the point.'

Becoming more serious in his pedagogy, Peter laid down his fork and pressed his fingertips together, 'Seeing the pictures *is* seeing the point. They're about *seeing*.' They all looked at him for a moment then Priscilla said, her voice soft with respect, 'That's what Harold says as well.' Peter smiled beatifically. After a further minute of silence, Rachel slipped quietly away to make the coffee.

It was after midnight when Beth and Jim, making apologies about a young babysitter, left the company. By unspoken agreement, Julian and Priscilla stayed on after they had gone, Jim and Beth being the sort of couple whom people wanted to discuss at the end of an evening.

'Christ,' Julian began, 'exhausting isn't it?' Rachel giggled next to him on the sofa. 'You have to admire him, really.'

Peter, handing round the brandy, concurred humanely. 'It's a kind of integrity. Heroic and really rather sad.'

'Really rather boring,' Julian persevered, unimpressed by Peter's display of charity. 'It's so dishonest,' he went on, 'he lives as affluent a life as anybody. He drives a BMW, for Christ's sake.'

'And Beth,' Priscilla added, her usual restraint loosened by alcohol, 'doesn't do anything. She's the perfect bourgeois housewife.' Rachel mused, 'They're fascinating, really, as a case study – middle-class Socialist circa late twentieth-century.'

'A museum piece,' Peter concluded her thought, laughing without malice. 'Never mind. Without that species, we could never have evolved.'

'Social Democrat Man, you mean?' Rachel asked, cheerfully including themselves in the parody. Julian sipped his brandy. 'The sooner you replace that lot, the better,' he said seriously.

'Never fear,' Peter replied, 'the more advanced evolutionary stages always get the upper hand in the end.'

'Let's hope it's in time for the country,' Rachel said, her eyes shining slightly with dedication. It was after two when Julian and Priscilla left. They returned to a quiet house, children and au pair soundly asleep, and sat in their own living room for a further half-hour of postmortem on the dinner party.

The evening out had been therapeutic for Julian. Although he had protested about the social obligation following on so quickly after his trip to New York, he had, in fact, been refreshed and enlivened by it, feeling less tired now than he had when they had left the house.

'You see,' Priscilla chided him, 'it wasn't so bad.' He smiled and shrugged somewhat grudgingly. 'Jim's always good entertainment value,' he admitted.

'How are you feeling?' she asked. He had been complaining of a headache and a sore throat that afternoon in the depths of his reluctance to keep the dinner engagement.

'I'm all right,' he said. 'Just jet lag.' She came to stand behind his chair, and put her hands on the back of his neck. He shut his eyes and leant back against her. Resting his head against the soft curve of her stomach, he felt dreamily sensual, wishing that he could remain in this pleasant state of mild arousal forever. Priscilla leant forward to say quietly, 'Coming to bed?' The sensation of her breath on his ear made his vague excitement more specific and imperative. He stood up and followed her upstairs.

His sleep patterns were still disturbed from two trips across the Atlantic in three days. Lassitude seemed constantly to be at odds with surprising flashes of wakefulness. He lay down on the bed still dressed and watched Priscilla as she took off her clothes, allowing the desire to stir comfortably in his groin. Then she slipped her nightgown over her head and disappeared into the bathroom. When she came back, he was wearing only his pyjama bottoms as he always did when he was planning to make love. He got into bed next to her and slipped his hand under the strap of her nightgown. 'You looked very pretty tonight,' he said. She smiled and put her arms around him, pulling his head down to kiss him properly for the first time since he had got home.

⋆ ⋆ ⋆

Priscilla offered her cheek to be kissed as Alfred Kingslade reached her through the crush.

'Super show,' he enthused. They were being forced into a corner against the plan chests at the back of the gallery. Harold's opening had attracted even larger numbers than the last time he had had a show in London four years ago. The atmosphere of excitement was building on itself as the crowd increased, its self-congratulatory clamour pressing against the ears. Alfred beamed at her, communicating the high spirits which infected everyone who felt a part of such an event. One of the middle generation of Tate trustees, he had been among the people responsible for the Tate's purchases of Harold's earlier paintings.

'Where is he?' Alfred asked.

'Hiding in the office, I think,' Priscilla replied. 'He hates private views, especially his own.'

'This show will do him a lot of good,' Alfred said, having to shout above the din. 'He's brought everything to fruition that he's been hinting at for years. The big ones are a marvellous development. He's really broken through.'

Priscilla nodded enthusiastically, squeezing to one side to allow one of their staff to pass carrying a tray full of wine glasses.

'Do go and have a word,' she said. 'I'm sure he'd love to see you.'

As Alfred eased his way back toward the office, Priscilla saw Simon beckoning to her from the other side of the room. She put her glass down on the plan chest, finding the prospect of making her way across the packed room with a full glass of wine too daunting. Half way to Simon, her arm was seized by Cyril Hartwell, the critic who had done most to promote Harold's work over the last ten years.

'Wonderful show,' he carolled, blinking from behind his red framed glasses. She smiled. 'Did you get in earlier to have a proper look?'

'No,' he said. 'Had to visit a chum in hospital this afternoon but I'll come in tomorrow. My deadline's not till Friday so I've got time to write it up. Where's the man himself?'

'In the office, trying to stay out of sight. Go and see him.'

'Oh, I won't pester him now. Do you think he could come in and have a little chat with me tomorrow when I'm making my notes?'

'I should think so. What time do you want to come in?'

'After lunch – about three?'

'Super. I'll let him know.'

Disengaging herself, she began the push once more towards the far wall. Finally breaking through to Simon's corner, she found him with a tall prepossessing man dressed, rather noticeably at this gathering, in a double-breasted grey suit. Priscilla always recalled later that she had been more struck on that first meeting by his clothes than by his looks. Simon grasped her elbow as soon as she was within reach.

'Priscilla, come and meet Alistair Thurston.' Turning to Thurston, he said, 'Priscilla handles our publicity now and she's done a lot of work on Harold's promotion.'

As Simon slipped away into the crowd, Thurston smiled at her with the engaging professional smile of a politician but his eyes searched her face with an interest that stopped just short of calculation. She returned his smile and said, 'You own some of Harold's pictures, don't you?'

'Yes, I do,' he replied warmly, never taking his eyes off her face. 'I bought him when he was in his earlier, pale phase.' Then he added, with no real contention but obviously as a conversational gambit, 'I'm not sure that I can get used to the new strong colours. It's a bit overwhelming for me.'

She felt herself slipping into her publicist's manner. 'Yes, it's quite a change. But he sees it as a progression – loosening up and losing his inhibitions. They're more courageous paintings, less cautious.' Thurston nodded, accepting her comments. 'It isn't just the colour,' he said. 'It's the form. The grids have disappeared. He's not so interested in geometry now.'

He noticed the surprise flicker across her face at the sophistication of his judgement and was gratified when her voice dropped its implied condescension. 'I do think there's something very strong about the new ones, especially as he's just finding his feet on this ground,' she said. Thurston glanced round the walls, tall enough to see over most of the heads in the room. 'The lithographs still look half way between the old and the new – more structured.'

'Yes, they do,' she said, aware that he was right and that it was something she had not noticed before. He turned fully to her and looked directly into her eyes, smiling benignly. 'How long have you been with the gallery?'

'A year full time,' she said. 'I'd done a bit of freelance public relations for them before that.'

'Have you always worked in the art world?'

She shook her head. 'I was in the publicity department at Thames Television for a while. Then I went freelance for a few years.'

'Do you like working for a gallery?'

'Oh, yes,' she said. 'It's good fun.'

'It must be awkward,' he said, with a teasing grin, 'if you have to promote work you don't particularly like. Or does that never happen?'

She shrugged. 'I didn't like all the programmes at Thames TV, either . . .' He smiled broadly and said, as confidentially as he could above the noise, 'Simon was telling me something about the Macmasters collection.' *My God*, she thought, *Simon doesn't waste any time.*

She looked at Thurston expectantly, wanting him to make clearer how much he had been told. Thurston gathered that she was waiting for him to go on and said, 'He thought Macmasters might be interested in giving them to the nation.'

'I think it's conceivable,' she said carefully. Thurston gave a look intended to make it plain that he was interested. 'How many of Harold's pictures has he got?'

'About a dozen, I think. There are some Ben Nicholsons and some Moore and Picasso drawings, and a few Rothkos.'

Thurston took it all in with polite seriousness. 'Are most of them very big?' he asked.

'Harold's and the Rothkos are. Not the others.'

Simon reappeared at her elbow with two glasses of wine and presented them with mock ceremoniousness to Thurston and herself. Tucked under his arm was a copy of the catalogue. 'Have you got one of these?' he asked, offering it to Thurston.

'Oh, no I haven't,' Thurston said, graciously pleased. Priscilla turned to Simon. 'It seems to be getting a good response.'

'Yes,' Simon said happily. 'If this atmosphere is anything to go by, it's going to be well received.' Thurston sipped his wine, making no move to bring the conversation to an end. Priscilla asked him, 'Do you buy many other painters?'

'I've got a couple of Hodgkins and some early Lucien Freuds,' he answered readily, pleased at her interest.

'Your tastes are quite varied.'

'I suppose they are, really. I've got quite a few nineteenth-century things as well. French, mostly.'

'Impressionists?'

'No, they're too expensive for me. Earlier.'

Simon was being called by a shout from the office and as he excused himself, Thurston looked at his watch. 'I'm afraid,' he said, 'that I'm going to have to get to the House.' He made a regretful face and said, 'Much less edifying than talking about paintings.' Then he looked at her. 'I'd quite like to talk about the Macmasters collection, some time.'

She was slightly taken aback by his alacrity. 'Fine,' she said, rather stupidly unable to think of anything to add. He touched her arm and said, 'Perhaps we can arrange to talk about it. Could you ring my private secretary at the Ministry and make a date?'

'Yes, I'll do that.' She beamed, relieved that the gallery would have time to get its position sorted out before she had to discuss it further.

'Could you say "good night" to Simon for me?' he asked pleasantly as he prepared to make his way toward the door.

'Of course,' she said and turned away herself to head for the office, anxious to tell Simon how well it had gone.

A small throng of people formed and reformed around the office door, first thinning into a stream which filed through in an excited procession, then widening to a broader mass which engulfed the space outside the entrance. This crowd, with its constant amoeba-like fluctuation of shape and its animated gaiety, was the queue attending upon Harold Lewis, who sat inside. Priscilla slipped through the outer perimeter of the group picking up the infectious elation of this party within a party – those who felt sufficiently close to the artist to justify a personal audience. Recognized as a member of the gallery's staff, a path was opened for her through the door. In an open-necked shirt and denim jacket, Harold reclined in Bertie's leather armchair, a glass of whisky in one hand while the other ran repeatedly through his shaggy, greying hair. Ranged around the office were an assortment of eagerly cheerful admirers, those most confident in their status seated with tranquil permanence on the sofa, followed by aspirants who perched less comfortably on desks or, at least leaned with unhurried complacency against filing cabinets. The frankly transient slid through the door in orderly turns to offer their salutations and participate for a brief moment in the aura, watched with patronizing indulgence by those acolytes more securely ensconced.

'Is there *really*,' Harold was saying, his hand stirring his hair energetically, 'a way to depict *time*. I mean, as soon as you have *real* space in a picture, you destroy time because it becomes a picture of one moment *in* time.' His interlocutor, a very young man with an insubstantial beard and long, thin legs, replied ardently, '*Exactly* – that's what I . . .'

'I mean,' Harold's voice strode on, 'reality has to be about time *and* space. People talk about real space as if that was all there was to reality but you have to include time as a dimension.'

'*Exactly*,' the young man blurted, 'that's what my work ...'

'Experience is really,' Harold continued, with all eyes in the room gazing at him, 'more about *time* as a dimension than space.' The young man, beside himself with fervour, rushed out, 'My painting is based on this whole thing about relativity – about time as a dimension of the universe.'

Priscilla, moving as unobtrusively as she could through the rapt assembly, approached Simon who stood beaming proprietorially behind Harold's chair. Catching his eye, she signalled at him that she wanted a word. He smiled blandly back at her, too immersed in the atmosphere of Harold's presence to pick up her cue. Deciding to wait for a more opportune moment, she took up a station near enough to Harold to note that seated on the floor at his feet was a pretty young girl with long straight hair and a happily open smile. Wearing white jeans and a white jumper, which looked to Priscilla like cashmere, she seemed blissfully aware of her privileged position, requiring no attentiveness from Harold himself to reinforce her contentment. Never having seen her before, Priscilla was mildly curious about the assured possessiveness with which she attached herself to Harold. Noticing that she did not have a glass, Priscilla leant over her shoulder and asked her quietly if she would like a drink. Turning with a radiantly sweet smile, she replied, 'Oh no, that's okay,' in an unmistakably American accent. Pushing her hair over her shoulder with a small, childlike hand, she smiled again at Priscilla with trusting friendliness.

Harold had paused in his monologue to sip his whiskey which permitted the attention of his audience to lapse into self-conscious sociability. Simon, stirring from his place behind Harold's chair, moved towards Priscilla. 'How did *you* get on?' he asked with a pointed grin, having noted how long her conversation with Thurston had continued.

'Very well,' she said. 'He's definitely interested.'

'I'm sure he is, dear,' Simon said with a toss of his head.

Priscilla made a dismissive face, 'He's just a professional charmer, that's all.'

There was a small eruption of movement around the door as the art critic of one of the Sunday papers passed through into the office, making it necessary for some of those close to Harold to rearrange themselves so that the new arrival could take his appropriate place. Harold's young American girlfriend sat sublimely unaffected by this reshuffling, his only acknowledgement of her presence consisting of a failure to be surprised by it.

★ ★ ★

They went for a meal after the private view. Priscilla took Simon and Bertie and one of Harold's entourage in her car. A booking had been made for eight people at the Chinese restaurant in the King's Road and their party was now twelve. In spite of this and the fact that they were nearly an hour later than expected, the head waiter accommodated them genially around an ad hoc arrangement of adjoining tables. Decanted from shared taxis, the rest of their group arrived, their conviviality swelling to fill the restaurant. The large green and white room resounded with the sound of their happy excitement as they moved toward their seats, watched with guarded curiosity by more self-effacing diners. They seated themselves around the L-shaped grouping of tables, calling to one another jovially. Harold and his girlfriend were the last to arrive, having taken a surprisingly long time to make the journey. Bertie cried, 'Here he is!' delightedly as Harold ambled toward them smiling impassively. The girl followed on behind, waiting with luxuriant serenity while places were found between Bertie and Priscilla. They sat down to a chorus of welcome, the girl smiling with recognition at Priscilla as she slipped gracefully into the chair next to her.

'I'm Priscilla Burford,' she said pleasantly, wanting the girl to introduce herself but she simply smiled once again and said warmly, 'Hi,' before lapsing into her pacific self-containment. Menus were distributed and the need to confer on the communal order caused further ripples of hilarity. Finally, Bertie carolled, 'Shall I do the ordering?' Someone at the end of the table called, 'Oh do, Bertie. We trust you.'

Harold's girlfriend gazed up at the slowly revolving fans hanging from the ceiling, then turned to Priscilla. 'This is a great place,' she said.

'Yes,' Priscilla said, 'it is nice.'

'It's a bit like places in Hong Kong,' the girl mused. Wanting to pursue the conversation, Priscilla asked, 'Have you been there recently?'

'Last year.'

'What were you doing there?' Priscilla asked agreeably.

'Just travelling. I wanted to go to China itself but I couldn't get a visa so I never got further than Hong Kong.'

'Gosh, that's adventurous. What did you want to do in China?'

'Well, write some articles about it, mainly. I knew I could sell pieces about China if I could get in.'

'Oh, are you a journalist?' Priscilla asked. The girl nodded. 'Who do you write for?'

'Lots of different places. Magazines mostly – travel pieces or interviews.' She smiled with pointed warmth. 'That's how I met Harold, by going to interview him.'

'Oh, really,' Priscilla replied. 'What's your name? Perhaps I've seen your piece.'

'It hasn't appeared yet. It's with the *Mail on Sunday* now and I think they're going to use it.'

'You must let me know when it's due to appear,' Priscilla said enthusiastically. 'We like to keep all the clippings on file.'

'Oh, I will,' the girl agreed.

The food began to arrive then and the whole party was once again convulsed in escalating high spirits as they passed dishes down the long tables. They lingered over the meal until after midnight, their noisy exuberance creating a festive atmosphere in the restaurant whose Chinese staff showed no signs of impatience as the rest of the large room emptied. Finally, they emerged onto the pavement, reluctant to disperse into the darkness. But as the coldness of the night began to penetrate the warmth of their collective good spirits, they headed in their respective directions, some managing to prolong companionship by sharing taxis or offering lifts.

It was nearly half-past one when Priscilla arrived home. The lights were still on downstairs. Julian had waited up. He was sitting in the living room reading reports when she came in.

'Long private view,' he said without looking up.

'I told you we'd be going for a meal afterwards,' she said, trying to avoid an apologetic whine.

'Long meal,' he muttered after a pause.

'It was very convivial,' she admitted, feeling the euphoria draining from her even as she described it. 'The opening was a great success and everybody wanted to celebrate.'

He said nothing and did not raise his eyes.

'How were the kids? Did they go off all right?' she asked, sitting down on the sofa opposite his chair. He nodded mutely, then added, 'Krista gave them tea and let them watch television for a while.' His voice was losing its coldness but he still had not looked at her.

'What time did you eat?' she asked.

'About eight. Waited till they'd gone to bed.'

She had left a casserole for the au pair to reheat, as she usually did when she was out for the evening. Although Julian did know how to cook, he usually reserved his more specialized skills for nights when they were entertaining.

'Do you want some tea?' she asked.

He could not hold out against this symbolic offering. He met her eyes now and nodded with terse pleasantness. Krista had left the basement kitchen impeccably well ordered, milk bottles washed and breakfast things laid. The small electronic illuminations of kitchen appliances glowed in the darkness, the digital clock on the wall oven, the green light at the top of the fridge freezer, the glowing red eye of the coffee machine left on. She switched off the coffee and filled the kettle. There was a sudden noise behind her as Pushkin banged through the cat flap. Having seen the kitchen light come on, he had obviously decided to come in from the cold and plead for food. Priscilla poured some of the top of the milk into his saucer and he wrapped himself around her ankles gratefully. She decided to make Earl Grey because it was Julian's favourite. She served it with slices of lemon in the way that he preferred and took it upstairs on a tray with some biscuits. At the sight of the tea tray, Julian put his reports away.

'It went well then, I take it,' he said with grudging civility as she poured out the tea.

Priscilla nodded, finding herself surprisingly reluctant to describe it in any detail. She was at home now and her domestic personality was taking over. She was unsure which side of herself it was she wished to protect from the other.

'How was your meeting?' she asked, inviting him to talk about his own day.

'Fine,' he smiled for the first time. 'We won.'

'Really?' she asked, genuinely pleased. 'There won't be a merger?'

He shook his head. 'We cornered the votes just in time. It was a clear majority in our favour.' She realized then that this was what he had been waiting up to tell her.

'Patterson must be pleased,' she said.

'Exceedingly,' he agreed. 'Positively ecstatic.'

'Will they expand now?'

He nodded, sucking absently on a slice of lemon as he always did. 'I should think so.' It occurred to her how much more she knew about his professional existence than he knew about hers. At any given moment, she was aware of most of the major concerns which would be occupying him even down to the details of his daily appointments. As they finished their tea, he smoothed his hand over her knee and said, 'It's after two. Shall we go to bed?'

She carried the tea tray downstairs and left it on top of the dishwasher, then climbed the two flights of stairs to join him.

* * *

'It's just a question of how far they can go without looking too squalid,' Thurston was saying, refilling their wine glasses.

'And how far you can go without being sacked,' Fitzjohn said mischievously.

Thurston smiled ruefully. 'We're all keeping a very low profile.' This lunch with Harry Fitzjohn was a risk, Alistair knew, but newspaper editors who enjoyed playing power politics could be useful go-betweens. If the general election due within a year did produce the expected hung Parliament then, as the golden boy of the Tory moderates, Thurston would be well placed to figure in a coalition government.

'They may yet do a deal with the comrades,' Fitzjohn ventured teasingly. Thurston knew that he was being sounded out and decided to play it for all it was worth. 'The buggers would only use it as a front. They'd knacker all those renegades just like they did when they were still in the party. They'd spend most of their time bickering about re-nationalization and discredit the Social Democrats by dragging them into the chaos. If I were with the Liberal lot, I'd throw in with us and take some of the credit for restructuring the economy the next time round.'

Harry smiled at the persuasiveness of this account, fully aware of Thurston's vested interest. Consensus politics and the exigencies of coalition could bring Tory wets like Thurston into an ascendancy they had not known for a decade.

'No real problems about defence, are there?' Fitz murmured.

'None that couldn't be ironed out,' Thurston replied, keeping his eyes on his Dover sole.

'What about,' Fitz mused, 'the dreaded PR?' Alistair pulled a face. 'They can quietly drop that, can't they? They won't need it to get in after the next time.'

Harry leaned back, smoothing his hand over his stomach complacently. He was vastly enjoying this role, Thurston knew, and helping him to play it could pay some future dividend if Fitzjohn had half the influence which he implied that he had. 'But it's their great democratic reform, isn't it – proportional representation,' Harry said doubtfully.

'But it isn't democratic at all, is it Harry? When you have guaranteed stalemate, the party with the smallest number of supporters ends up calling the tune.' Fitzjohn smiled and put his hands up. 'Don't argue with me. It's their policy – talk them out of it.'

As their coffee arrived, Thurston said, 'I can't see them doing any sort of deal with Labour now. It's too far gone.'

Harry shrugged. 'Nothing is irreversible. They need time – a couple of years in office with a coalition and they might sort out the constituency parties and get back on the rails.'

'It's not time they need, it's balls.'

'But if the country gets disenchanted with utopian capitalism ...' Harry thought aloud. Thurston looked at his watch. 'I'm afraid I'm going to have to move. I've got a very charming lady coming to see me.'

'How nice.' Harry smiled generously. 'Business or pleasure?'

'Hopefully both,' Thurston said.

They took leave of each other on the corner of Regent Street where Thurston hailed a taxi. As Fitzjohn watched him being driven away he thought with amused admiration that Thurston was the sort of man who never had to wait long for a taxi, or anything else for that matter.

It was an enormous building, deceptive from its front entrance. The Department of the Environment, in fact, occupied a row of buildings all of which adjoined so that the corridors seemed to stretch beyond the visible horizon. Priscilla had only a few moments to wait in the lobby downstairs before being conducted to the lift by a pleasantly attentive member of Thurston's staff. The grey-suited young man guided her round several corners on the fifteenth floor, past anonymous clerical offices, through swing doors, finally emerging into a large outer office whose décor was less institutional than the corridor from which they had entered. This room held four desks, three of which were occupied. Its furnishings were utilitarian and modern, rather than sumptuous in the way that a private office of such a degree of importance would be.

Thurston's aide slipped decorously past her to knock on the door of the inner room. Priscilla heard him say, 'Mrs Burford is here, Minister.'

Then the door was opened by another member of staff and she was ushered into Thurston's presence. Here, surrounded by the apparatus of his office, Thurston seemed a more formidable figure than the amiable aesthete he had appeared at the gallery. He smiled, not so much charming now as benevolent, and left his desk to greet her. She had not remembered being aware at their first meeting of how tall he was. He seemed to tower over her as he led her to the comfortable chairs grouped in the corner of his office. Decorated to his taste, the room was painted in an indeterminate muted colour, its walls hung with small paintings and a few prints. Priscilla glanced round and then saw Thurston smile as he noticed her taking in the pictures.

'They're not all mine,' he said. 'Some of them belong to the government.'

'Which ones are yours?' she asked because she knew the interest would flatter him. He pointed to two small French landscapes, probably mid-nineteenth-century, and a Lucien Freud portrait.

'A few of the lithographs, as well,' he said, motioning toward some abstract prints.

She nodded appreciatively, giving his own works prolonged attention.

'It's a very nice Freud,' she commented.

'I'm particularly fond of that one,' he said, obviously pleased. 'Bought it years ago when he was still with the Marlborough. I don't think I could afford him now.'

'Yes,' she agreed. 'His prices have shot up.'

'Harold's, too,' he said. She looked at him quickly, wondering how knowing the remark was. But his expression was benign, his eyes she realized now, holding her face intently. He dropped his gaze as she turned toward him.

'Would you like some tea?' he asked solicitously. She accepted politely and he made an almost imperceptible gesture with his head to the aide who had discreetly moved to the far side of the office and who now vanished with silent efficiency to conjure up their tea.

Thurston leaned back in his chair and crossed his legs as if to signify that, with the summoning of tea, the interview had reached a plateau of informality.

'Ghastly building, isn't it?' he said, congenially.

'It's certainly vast,' she admitted.

'Worst sort of post-war modern,' he grimaced. 'Completely faceless. It's the older Ministries that have the nice buildings.'

She smiled and wondered whether he coveted a more prestigious ministerial job purely out of architectural preference.

'I've had a few thoughts about Macmasters,' he began, looking at her expectantly to see if there was anything she wanted to say at the outset.

'We've had some discussions with him on the subject,' she

said carefully. She went on, 'He definitely likes the idea of presenting the collection to the nation but he's very concerned that it be kept together.'

Thurston nodded. 'That's understandable.'

The tea tray appeared, gliding unobtrusively across the room supported by a young woman. Thurston poured out the tea himself. As he handed her a cup with a smile that was almost ingratiating in its courtesy, she was struck, in a disinterested way, by how good looking he was. The ageing film star face of a diplomat, she thought. He sipped his tea slowly, making it clear that their conversation need not be hurried.

'The problem,' he said, 'is finding a home for them, isn't it?'

'Yes,' she said, 'and then deciding on the details of their upkeep. Macmasters would consider setting up a trust to take care of the maintenance and insurance but he's rather worried about the cost of the housing. He'd like to know,' she concluded with tactful vagueness, 'if we could come to some arrangement with the government on it.'

Thurston looked interested but dubious. 'Possibly ...' he said slowly, 'we'll really have to discuss all this with the Arts Minister, I think. Money is pretty scarce these days, especially for open-ended commitments.' Then he added, 'And I assume that this would be an indefinite undertaking. Macmasters would make it a proviso of the gift that the collection could never be broken up, wouldn't he?'

'I should think he would,' Priscilla said, drinking her tea.

Thurston retired into a thoughtful silence. After a moment, he looked directly into her eyes and smiled, 'I think that what we shall have to do is set up a meeting with the Arts Minister and his Permanent Secretary. I'll try to arrange it sometime within the next couple of weeks. Can you represent Macmasters yourself in negotiations?'

'Only informally. For anything official, I'd need his solicitor there.'

'Oh, I doubt that we'll get to that stage for a while,' Thurston assured her. He thought again for a moment, then said, 'Let me sound out the Arts Ministry to begin with. Then perhaps you and I can get together and I'll brief you on what to expect when we have a proper meeting.'

'That would be terribly kind of you,' she said warmly.

Delighted that she was losing her reserve, Thurston dropped his voice to a more intimate tone, 'You must come in some time to see the picture collection the Environment Ministry has. They've got some amazing things that they circulate around the public buildings. The best ones never seem to get hung anywhere where anyone can see them.'

'Do they have many contemporary things?' she asked.

'Not all that many. Partly, I think, because they find it hard to get good advice about buying new work.' He grinned at her then and said, 'Perhaps you could offer your services as a consultant.'

She laughed but said nothing, unsure of how seriously she was to take this remark. He took her failure to rise to the overture as a retreat from him and knew that she was keeping her distance.

'Do you think he's likely to be sympathetic?' she asked.

'Malvern? I'm not sure, really. I don't think he has any particularly marked prejudices. His own interests are more theatre and opera than painting. I've never really discussed this sort of thing with him. I should think that, in principle, he'll be helpful but it will all come down to what his civil servants tell him about what kind of precedent he'll be establishing in making a financial undertaking.'

Priscilla sighed. It was all going to be, as she should have expected, terribly delicate and time-consuming. Her first flush of euphoria over Thurston's interest was slowly expiring as she faced the mass of bureaucratic complexities which would have to be overcome.

'Don't look so downhearted,' he said, his voice almost tender in its gentleness. She was startled by his tone, rather as if he had crept up on her stealthily and was suddenly disturbingly close. She smiled and he found her demure self-consciousness so powerfully seductive that his groin actually stirred. Recovering his poise, he said, 'It's not as bad as all that. I'm sure we can come to some sort of happy arrangement given everyone's goodwill.'

She nodded, pleased to accept his reassurance. 'Is there

anything more you want me to find out from Macmasters at this stage?'

She was looking down at the tea tray as she slid her empty cup on to it and he took the opportunity to let his eyes skim over her body. Glancing away quickly as she looked up, he said, 'As much detail as you can about what he would expect, really. If you can tell me what he's likely to want and I can find out what we're able to offer, we can thrash out some proposals between us to put to all the parties.' He grinned at her conspiratorially.

'Fine,' she said. 'I'll do that.'

A head appeared around the door and the aide who had shown her in said, 'Excuse me, Minister. Mr Wynne is here.'

Thurston looked at his watch and said, 'All right, tell him I'll just be a minute.' As the aide vanished, Thurston turned to her and said in a voice that conveyed real regret, 'Sorry, that's my PPS come to drag me off to the House. We'll have to arrange for a longer talk next time. Perhaps we can meet for lunch when I've had a chance to talk to Malvern.'

She stood up quickly, not wanting to delay him and said, 'Simon and I will have a proper talk with Macmasters as well and get as much firm information as we can.'

'Good.' He held her gaze warmly. Walking her to the door, he was tempted to touch her shoulder but found himself, to his mild alarm, seized by an adolescent shyness. He watched her leave through the outer office, directed to the lift by a member of his staff as Harvey Wynne bustled into the room with an armful of folders. Shutting the door as Harvey began sorting through his papers, Thurston said quietly, 'Oh, dear.' Wynne looked up inquisitively.

'I'm in real trouble,' Thurston murmured wryly.

'What's up?' Wynne asked. Thurston smiled and shook his head to imply that he wasn't serious and went to join Wynne at the desk.

* * *

It was nearly dark by the time she got back to the gallery at half-past four, the overcast of the afternoon bringing the day to a swifter end than would be expected in early March. The receptionist smiled at her as she came through the door.

'Is Simon in?' she asked immediately, eager to talk about her visit to the Ministry. As well as the hope which the meeting seemed to promise, there was a vague excitement connected with Thurston. Something of his proximity, his manner, seemed to be hovering over her as if his eyes were still on her. It was discomfiting, making her restless with self-consciousness and she wanted to discharge her agitation in the kind of animated conversation which she knew she could have with Simon. The receptionist pointed toward the office and Priscilla rushed toward it, meeting Simon as he emerged.

'Well,' he said, 'you are looking pleased with yourself.'

'Am I?' she asked, surprised. She had not understood her state of mind to be clearly pleasurable.

'It must have gone well,' he said with a grin.

'Oh, it did, I think,' she said, leading him back into the office. 'He's being very helpful.'

'Great,' Simon declared, falling in with her enthusiasm as she had known that he would.

'He's going to set up a meeting with the Arts Minister. There'll be a lot of bureaucratic wrangling but he seems to think that we can pull it off.' For some reason, she realized that she was reluctant to speak Thurston's name.

'That's fantastic,' Simon exclaimed. 'Should we contact Macmasters' solicitors, do you think?'

'Not yet,' she said. 'That would be premature, but we could tell him that we've had a very favourable response from the Ministry. It might make him inclined to meet them more than half way.'

'Oh yes,' Simon agreed. 'He'll be wildly flattered by all this to-ing and fro-ing with the government. Bertie will have to take him out to lunch next week.'

She sat down at her desk, fingering a pile of envelopes absently. 'He's willing to sound Malvern out and give us some advance warning of how he'll react. Perhaps we'd better wait until we've heard from him before saying anything to Macmasters.'

'Right. I'll tell Bertie to put it on hold for a bit. Does Thurston appreciate the urgency? Politicians have a way of forgetting what promises they've made by the end of the week.'

'I don't think he will,' Priscilla said cautiously, realizing that, in fact, she was absolutely confident that Thurston would not forget his promise to her, for reasons which she was reluctant to examine.

Pippa, the receptionist, put her head round the office door and looked at Priscilla. 'Debbie Ackerman is here asking for you.'

'Who?'

Pippa went *sotto voce.* 'That American girl who's going around with Harold.'

'Really?' Priscilla said, standing up. 'Where is she?' Pippa gestured to the front of the gallery. Priscilla came out of the office and looked down the length of the gallery toward the door. As soon as she appeared, Debbie, who had been waiting diffidently at the reception desk, smiled and walked forward to meet her.

'Hi,' she said with her engaging openness. 'Remember me?'

Priscilla smiled as well, her elation of the moment making her more cordial than she might otherwise have been. 'Of course I remember you,' she said. Debbie seemed very pleased by this reception. 'Sorry to bother you. Are you very busy right now?' she asked, making it clear that she wanted a fairly extended conversation.

'No, I'm not,' Priscilla said, leading the way into the office. 'Come in and sit down.' Debbie sat herself on the sofa, drawing her legs up under her as Simon slipped discreetly out into the gallery. There was something in Debbie's exclusive concentration on Priscilla which implied that she wished to talk to her privately. Priscilla sat at her desk, turning round on her revolving chair to face Debbie. Her white jeans had been replaced by a brown leather skirt but the soft white jumper remained.

'I wanted to ask you,' she began. 'You know that interview I told you about with Harold ...' Priscilla nodded receptively.

'Well, I think it might help to sell it if I had some photographs to go with it.'

'Yes,' Priscilla agreed. 'They always like to have visuals, don't they?'

Debbie looked happily relieved by Priscilla's alacrity. 'We've got the shots we used for the catalogue,' Priscilla said. 'Black and white mostly.' Then she added, 'Does Harold have any preference about which paintings he'd want used?'

Debbie looked vague. 'Oh, I don't really know. Perhaps you should ask him first.' Priscilla looked up in surprise, was about to ask why Debbie had not discussed it with him herself, then with almost subliminal insight, gathered from Debbie's awkwardness that she was not in touch with Harold at the moment. To dispel the embarrassment, Priscilla stood up purposefully and walked to the filing cabinet. 'Let's see what we've got here,' she said, opening the photograph drawer.

'I suppose,' Debbie ventured, 'he'd want the latest paintings to go in. He's so excited about those.'

Priscilla murmured agreement as she sorted through the glossy prints in Harold's file. Picking out four good photographs of the most recent works, she turned back to Debbie who sat curled in a corner of the sofa. Handing them to her, she asked, 'Will these do?'

Barely glancing at them, Debbie replied, 'Oh, they're fine.' She made no move to go and so Priscilla returned to her own chair and asked, 'Will it be going into the *Mail on Sunday*?' Debbie shook her head. 'They didn't think there would be enough interest among their readers. I'm going to try the colour supplements now.'

'The *Observer* did a piece last month in their Review section,' Priscilla pointed out in a helpful voice.

'Oh, yes, they did,' Debbie said immediately. 'I'll have to send it to the *Sunday Times*.' Her interest in pursuing this subject seemed to slacken but she was obviously intending to stay. Priscilla wondered if there was something else that she wished to ask or whether she was simply at a loose end. Art galleries often attracted people who wanted to linger and fraternize.

'You don't know,' Debbie said suddenly, 'when Harold's getting back from France, do you?'

'Is he in France?' Priscilla asked, surprised.

Debbie nodded. 'He said he needed a break after getting the show launched. He was completely exhausted. He needed,' she said sympathetically, 'to be completely alone for a while.'

'Yes,' Priscilla said. 'I can imagine that. After all the razzamatazz of the opening.' She continued, her mood making her more effusive than normal, 'There has been a lot of interest in his work. We had a Cabinet minister at the opening.' She wondered then why she had said that, what had made her want to refer to Thurston again.

'Really?' Debbie exclaimed. Then she asked, 'Which one was he?' Finding herself embarrassed at having to describe him, Priscilla glanced away and said, 'The very tall man in a dark grey suit.'

'Oh, I think I know,' Debbie said. 'I remember noticing him because he looked different from everyone else. He was very good looking,' she added enthusiastically.

Priscilla made a noise of guarded agreement. Debbie asked, 'Does he like Harold's work?

'Yes, he's bought some of his paintings in the past.'

'Really?' Debbie said with artless incredulity. Priscilla smiled. 'Why does that surprise you?'

'Oh, it's not that,' Debbie replied. 'It's just a funny thing about this country. I mean – everything connects with everything else. I worked in an art gallery in New York and I never saw any politicians. But here everybody seems to know everybody else. When you get to know an artist, you meet people in the government. I went to a party with this guy who teaches at London University and there were people there from the newspapers and publishing. It's funny how easy it is to meet people here. They all go to the same places.'

Priscilla smiled. 'I suppose,' she said, 'that's because everything happens in London.'

'Maybe,' Debbie said seriously. 'But even in New York, it's not like that. People tend to know their own circle. You don't get the feeling that everybody who's important knows everybody else who's important.'

'Oh, I'm not sure that's true,' Priscilla countered mildly.

'Well, not exactly,' Debbie agreed. 'But it does seem a bit like that.' Never having lived outside England, this description was meaningless to Priscilla because she could not contrast the social life she knew with any other. Life was simply as it was with all of the expectations one would consider normal.

'It really is,' Debbie mused again, 'incredibly easy to meet people here.' Priscilla was still rather sceptical of this observation but then it occurred to her that she herself had just had tea with a government minister, a reflection to which she seemed determined to return.

Simon peered in at the door and said apologetically, 'We're locking up now.' Debbie looked at her watch. 'Oh, it is five-thirty, isn't it?' She stood up, gathering up the photographs Priscilla had given her.

'Would you like an envelope for those?' Priscilla asked her.

'Oh, that would be great,' Debbie said gratefully. She pulled her jacket on as Priscilla slipped the prints into a manila envelope. Taking them from her, Debbie smiled and said, her voice warm with friendship, 'Thanks a lot. I've really enjoyed talking to you.' Priscilla, touched by her overture, responded in kind, 'That's all right. Come in again some time.'

'Oh, I will,' Debbie replied eagerly. Then, offering her broad smile to Simon as well, she said, 'Bye,' and left the office. When they had watched her go, Simon said, 'Sweet girl.'

'Mmm,' Priscilla murmured. Then she asked, 'Has Harold gone to France?'

'He went for a few days after the opening,' Simon said, 'but he's been back for a week.'

'Oh, dear,' Priscilla said quietly while Simon carried on turning out lights and locking the gallery's rear doors.

* * *

'Having a little flirt with the middle ground are you, old boy?' Malvern grinned at Thurston over his glass of malt whisky. Alistair winced and allowed Malvern the satisfaction of rendering him speechless.

'Don't worry, dear. Your secret's safe with me. We all have to take out the odd insurance policy, don't we?'

Alistair smiled uncomfortably. 'Just a toe in the water, nothing more.'

'Of course, of course,' Malvern chortled, delighted that he had hit home with what had been nothing more than a wild guess. He meant Thurston no malice, simply enjoyed teasing him, watching his pretty, boyish face become slightly tremulous with anxiety. But he was happy to change the subject and release Thurston from his hook. Malvern crossed his legs and leaned back in the leather chair which had followed him from one minor ministerial office to another over the years. As Minister for the Arts, he had licence to surround himself with rather more pretty things than would have been acceptable in his previous posts as under secretary for Health or Social Services. Talking about pension levels or numbers of national health service beds from an office bedecked with paintings and precious objects would not have done. It was pleasant now to work in a milieu which seemed more like an extension of his own home. Ensconced here amidst his prints and pieces of curving bronze and glass, he felt that he had reached his spiritual resting place. He beamed at Alistair with real warmth and said sweetly, 'Now tell me all about this problem you wanted to discuss.'

Alistair heard himself exhale a small sigh of relief as he relaxed into Malvern's affectionate intimacy. 'You've probably heard something,' he began tentatively, 'about Macmasters.' Malvern's face flickered with mischievous amusement, 'Aah, yes. There has been a little whisper.'

Thurston polished off the last of his whisky and Malvern immediately topped up his glass. Alistair signalled for him to stop but Malvern waved aside his protestations, anticipating with pleasure a serious drinking session to accompany what was clearly going to be a very good gossip. Resigning himself to the fact that Malvern's sympathetic assistance was probably worth a hangover, Alistair went on, 'He's talking about selling his entire contemporary collection, apparently.'

'All at once?' Malvern's eyes widened. Thurston nodded. 'Oh, dear,' Malvern tutted. 'That will be bad news for a lot of people.' Thurston said, 'Yes, Harold Lewis's gallery is very worried.'

'That's dear old Bertie Houghton, isn't it? Haven't seen him for years,' Malvern said with real concern.

Thurston nodded again. 'Macmasters has over a dozen of Lewis's biggest paintings. They'd never maintain their prices if he sold them all off at once.'

Malvern shook his head sadly. 'Would Bertie's gallery survive it?' Alistair sipped his whisky and shrugged. 'It would hit them very hard.'

Bevis extracted two small cigars from his breast pocket and offered one to Alistair. Although he smoked rarely these days, he accepted more out of gratitude for Bevis's hospitality than expected pleasure. He used the time it took to accept Bevis's light and draw a first deep inhalation, to decide his next gambit. But Bevis was already musing, 'Been terribly helpful to me in the past, Bertie. Got me a marvellous German expressionist picture once, *very cheap*.' His lips pursed. 'Rather naughty. He undervalued a collection that was offered to him, then sold most of it for vast amounts of money but let a couple of them go at a low price to a few *special friends*.' He winked at Alistair who smiled, inordinately pleased at the promising turn this conversation was taking.

'What's your interest in this, anyway? You don't collect on a big scale, do you?' Bevis asked amiably, refilling his own glass. It was Alistair who looked deliberately conspiratorial now because he knew that it would please Bevis and the whisky was making him toy happily with indiscretion. 'My interest is more personal,' he said with a mysterious smile.

'Aah,' Bevis grinned. 'Well then, what can we do about this nasty business?' Thurston took another deep pull on his cigar, enjoying the taste of it more than he had expected. 'The gallery have got Macmasters quite interested in the idea of offering the collection to the nation as a gift.'

Malvern chuckled at the brilliance of it. 'Clever old Bertie.'

'The problem is,' Alistair went on, but Malvern was ahead of him. 'Where the hell would we put them?' he said, anticipating Thurston's next remark. Alistair pulled a wry face acknowledging Bevis's acuteness. Then he said, 'Macmasters would consider helping out with the cost of housing them but we'd have to come to some arrangement for the government to share the cost so that it would be seen as an acquisition by the nation of a prestigious collection.'

'The Macmasters Collection,' Bevis announced with mock grandeur.

'Exactly,' Thurston said.

There was a knock. Malvern's Principal Private Secretary put his head round the door. With an apologetic nod to Thurston, he addressed his minister with a faint obsequiousness which approached self-parody. 'Do you need the Crosby papers for tomorrow morning, Minister?' Bevis adopted his look of endearing vagueness. 'Oh gosh, I can't remember. Ask Hopkins. He always knows the schedule.' Then he called, just as the Secretary's head had disappeared, 'Do come here, Charles. We need your advice.' Charles reappeared instantly.

'Come and sit down,' Malvern said warmly. Charles pulled up a chair to join them, declining Malvern's offer of a whisky.

'What sort of precedent do we have for accepting gifts of large collections of paintings?' Malvern began expansively, lighting another cigar.

'For the museums, Minister?' Charles asked helpfully.

'No,' Malvern said. 'This collection is too big for any of the museums and it would have to be kept together so it would need its own site.' Charles made a thoughtful face. 'I'm not sure that there are any direct precedents. I daresay we could find out.' Then he ventured carefully, 'What sort of scale of government contribution are we talking about?'

Bevis looked at Alistair expectantly who said, 'Excellent question. I really don't know. If we could make a public building available, we might be talking about very little actual cash. On the other hand, we may be discussing going halves on a property to be bought and maintained by some trust that Macmasters would set up.'

'Rather a sticky problem,' Malvern turned to his secretary confidentially. 'This collection could come up on the market if it isn't taken by the country. It would knock the stuffing out of the value of the works if they all went up for sale.'

'Oh, dear,' Charles murmured sympathetically.

'Absolutely disastrous for a number of terribly nice people,' Bevis went on in his most solicitous voice.

'I can look into the legalities if you like,' Charles offered smoothly.

'That would be very helpful,' Alistair said, beginning to feel profoundly sanguine about what he would be able to report to Priscilla on the telephone. Charles excused himself with promises of further information and Alistair finished his whisky, fending off with more determination this time Bevis's attempts to refill his glass yet again.

'Well,' Bevis said cheerfully, 'I think we should be able to get somewhere on this, don't you?'

'I certainly hope so,' Alistair replied with more fervour than he would have permitted himself if he had not been slightly drunk. He looked at his watch then, realized that it was half-past six and that he was due at a dinner at half-past seven. He stood up, a bit dizzy from the combined effects of the whisky on an empty stomach and the unfamiliar cigar.

'Must be off, Bevis,' he said warmly. 'Thanks for all the help. I'll arrange for a meeting with the gallery people and perhaps we can do some serious negotiating.'

'Right-o,' Bevis said, rising with him. As Alistair turned toward the door, Bevis winked at him and said, 'Good luck with whomever.'

★ ★ ★

Harvey Wynne collapsed into one of the most comfortable chairs in Thurston's office, exhausted after four days of late sittings and a frenetic amount of committee work. Alistair sat opposite him, looking nearly as fresh as he had on Monday morning, only a slight pallor betraying the exhaustion they all felt after a crippling week. He was pouring out tea, anything stronger being prohibited by the prospect of the drive back to their constituencies for the weekend. For Harvey, it was only a comfortable journey to Buckinghamshire but Alistair had to face a five-hour marathon to North Yorkshire where his safe seat lay amidst the sheep farms and villages of the Dales' county set. He always hoped to get away from London by four on the Fridays before constituency weekends in order to beat the rush hour and arrive home in time for a late supper. It was three-fifteen now. He might just make it.

'What have you got on this weekend?' Harvey asked, accepting his tea.

'Local party dinner dance on Saturday night . . . some people to lunch on Sunday, I expect,' Alistair mused absently, his voice sounding flat with resignation. Harvey glanced at his face. He was either more tired than he looked, or rather distracted. Thurston made no move to continue, so Harvey decided to enliven the conversation, 'Constituency party not going to get edgy about your diversions, are they?'

Thurston's head shot round. *Aah, there's a spark of life*, Wynne thought. Alistair shook his head, 'They're pragmatic types up there. Don't like all these hard-line parvenues much, anyway.' Taking on a parodied Colonel Blimp delivery, he went on, 'Conservatism has always been about practical politics, old man.' He sipped his tea and murmured, 'Ideology is altogether too gauche. They like their hay dry and their Tories damp.'

Wynne wondered whether Thurston was as confident as he pretended. Playing a double game might be worth a gamble in these strange times but it had to be a strain on the nerves. Alistair put his cup down and ran a hand through his hair. The telephone on his desk rang and Wynne saw Thurston look up hopefully as its extension was answered in the outer office. A few seconds later the door opened and a head appeared round it. 'Mrs Burford is on the phone, Minister.'

Thurston stood up quickly and walked to his desk. He had left a message at the gallery that morning for Priscilla, and as the time approached when he must leave for Yorkshire, he had grown more impatient for her to return his call. Her voice was friendly and familiar, perhaps because of the good news he was able to report about Malvern's response or perhaps, he thought grimly, because she felt less guarded when he was at the far end of a telephone line. In either event, he made as much use as he could of her pleased surprise, sharing the good fortune as co-conspirator.

'I think,' he said, catching her at the height of her enthusiasm 'that we ought to meet and get the parameters straight before any official negotiations, don't you?' She agreed cheerfully and he suggested lunch the following Tuesday. He would come and collect her at the gallery. Saying goodbye, he wished her a pleasant weekend and rang off feeling as if the warmth of her voice were circulating through his bloodstream. Wynne stood up from his chair on the far side of the office and Thurston started, having nearly forgotten that he was in the room. Wynne gave him a look of mildly amused reproach, 'Thought you looked vaguely preoccupied.'

Thurston smiled, flushed with relief that he could get

through a rather deadly weekend with this secret anticipated excitement in a corner of his mind. He stood up himself now, able to contemplate with greater energy the necessary feats of organization which had to be accomplished before he could leave.

★ ★ ★

It was nearly ten by the time he turned into their private road set deep in the lap of the Dales before they rose to meet the Yorkshire Moors. A small early Victorian country house surrounded by a respectable but modest amount of land, his home suited the tastes he had been encouraged to acquire by an ambitious doctor father and a socially aspiring mother. Leaving behind his middle-class roots had been facilitated by the Yorkshire Young Conservatives' happy willingness to act as a marriage bureau for the more acceptable sons of local professionals. His engagement to Katherine Hunterton-Clarke had had as its only blemish his failure to be a Roman Catholic but her family, counting the assets of Alistair's political promise and considerable charm, accepted this with good grace excusing him conversion so long as he did not interfere with the religious upbringing of their grandchildren. His professional rise and increasing comfortableness in his social position had more than rewarded their generosity. Their daughter, Kate, had proved a competent constituency wife, leading pretty much the sort of social life she would have expected to lead whomever she had married, but with increased status. Her upbringing, free of suburban proprieties, had provided her with the degree of detachment necessary to make few enquiries about the rest of her husband's life. If forbearance had turned to cynicism in recent years, it was handled with discretion. She had her house, her social circle and her sons at Ampleforth and one had to keep these things in proportion.

Supper had been kept for him in the kitchen and he ate it from his lap by the open fire in the small sitting room. He was genuinely exhausted now and very hungry, having made the drive without a stop. It was considerably colder up here than in London and there was snow on the ground. The drop in temperature always took him by surprise when he drove north.

Kate sat opposite him while he ate. 'How are you?' she asked in that faintly distant way of hers.

'All right,' he said civilly, 'rather tired.'

'Harrogate tomorrow night,' she said.

He nodded and glanced heavenward in mild protestation. 'It's never as bad as you expect,' she countered. He suspected that she rather enjoyed, if not the actual occasions, at least the attention and glamour which attached to themselves at these provincial blow-outs.

'What else?' he asked.

'Nothing tomorrow, except Felix coming round in the afternoon about the trees. Mortons and Lindsays to lunch on Sunday. Nothing on Sunday evening. Richard said no surgery this time because of the weather but could you ring him, he needs a fairly lengthy chat.'

Alistair laid his empty plate down on the coffee table, acknowledging all of her information with a glance. 'Any coffee?'

'It's late to drink coffee,' she pointed out.

'Nothing would keep me awake.'

She went to the kitchen to get his coffee and he leaned back on the sofa and shut his eyes. When a cup appeared on the table in front of him almost instantaneously, he realized that he must actually have fallen asleep.

'How are the boys?' he asked as he sipped his coffee.

'Fine. Adrian is making his option choices next term so we'll have to manage a visit to see the Head quite soon.'

'Both of us?'

'It would be best, if you can.' She went on, 'You'll be pleased to hear that we've got the back wall sorted out. It wasn't dry rot. Keevers have seen to it and given us a twenty-year guarantee on the work.'

'Good,' he said, more relieved at this news than his fatigue would permit him to show. His favourite Labrador bitch, Winnie, wandered into the room and accosted him happily, putting her front paws on his knees. He smiled and scratched her head which produced another burst of affection. He had to stop her forcibly from bounding up to lick his face. Alistair rubbed his eyes and said, 'Sorry, I'm going to have to get to bed. I can't stay awake any longer.'

She nodded, 'All right. What time do you want to be got up in the morning?'

'Not before ten,' he said, disengaging himself from the dog so that he could leave the room to go upstairs.

* * *

Kate was wearing a royal blue taffeta dress with long sleeves, the sort of garment she would not have worn in London but which suited the expectations of the local gentry and their striving imitators. She brushed a speck of fluff from Alistair's shoulder with unselfconscious proprietoriness and he smiled at her, enjoying the confidence he felt in his own appearance. It struck him how much less frequently he was called on to wear black tie in London than he was in Yorkshire. The midwinter dinner dance was a mainstay of local Conservative social life and although anticipation of it paralysed him with boredom, he usually managed to glide through it on the automatic pilot with which politicians of any experience were equipped.

'Ready?' he asked Kate. She nodded and pulled her fur jacket around her, preparing to brave the freezing wind outside. The drive to Harrogate would take no more than forty minutes. He would drive there and she would drive back so that he would be free to indulge in as much conviviality as his supporters would expect.

As their Jaguar pulled up in front of the hotel whose main ballroom was hired every year for the occasion, there was a surge from the eager welcoming party which milled expectantly in the front lobby. A flurry of furs and dinner jackets, a burst of jovial recognition and they were descended upon, happily enveloped in their entrance by familiar and would-be familiar faces. Swept into the bar which was closed to everyone except their party this evening, they were bought their first drinks by his agent, Tommy Morton. The slow, regal progress through the bar emerged finally at the entrance to the ballroom. A wide crescent of tables, covered in white linen tablecloths, each with a small spray of flowers and two silver candlesticks, encircled the polished wooden dance floor. The platform with its folding chairs and music stands waited vacantly for the band to make its entrance. Their table was, as always, in the centre of the semicircle and it sat eight. They would be joined this year by Tommy Morton and his wife, the constituency party chairman, Charles Hillier and his daughter, and two of the most generous local contributors to party funds and their wives. Hillier's daughter often acted as an escort for him in his widowhood. She had grown up considerably since Alistair had last seen her and now promised at least a piquant aesthetic distraction in the *longueurs*. A deeply scooped neckline on a velvet dress which clung becomingly to her narrow waist provided a pleasant vision across the table and Alistair found himself rationing his gaze in that direction early in the evening. What the barons around the table wanted from him was political gossip, allowing them to feel like the insiders they were not, and what their wives required were his flattering attentions. Coping fairly expertly with both, Thurston floated through the presentable meal provided with a generous enough flow of wine to keep the mood mellow and the jokes well-received. The speeches were endured, and the dancing begun by Kate and himself. He then danced in turn with each of the wives at his table and finally, with some relish, took Annabel Hillier to the floor. It was a pleasure to feel the small, tautness of her waist against his hand and he had to fight back an impulse to kiss the soft curve of her neck, not with any actual sexual intention but simply out of sensual delight in her youth and honest liveliness.

'You must find all this monumentally boring,' he smiled down at her. She looked at him with a more knowing expression than he would have expected and shook her head.

'Wouldn't you prefer to be with people your own age?' he persevered.

She smiled at him and said, with a look of inviting warmth, 'Some of the time.'

Her flirtation was almost naive in its openness and he wondered whether it was an actual offer or simply a young girl's tease. Either way, it was academic. He would never insult his wife by indulging in any horseplay locally. His London life was in another compartment altogether from his situation at home where he upheld, rather quaintly perhaps, a code of honourable behaviour. He fell silent for the rest of their dance leaving Annabel to wonder whether he was rejecting or pondering her invitation. Towards midnight, voices became more booming, laughter more raucous and postures more relaxed as people milled about the room, many taking their opportunity to sit for a few minutes in the presence of the Junior Minister, occupying as much of his time as they felt their position in the hierarchy permitted. Repeating many of the same Westminster anecdotes, listening with as convincing a version of rapt attention as he could manage, Thurston got through the next two hours supported by alcohol and invincible poise. Shortly after two, it seemed conceivable to leave and he signalled to Kate with an almost imperceptible facial expression that he had had enough. She rose instantly and began making gracious exit noises to the small assemblage of people gathered on her side of the table. Alistair felt a warm rush of gratitude for her reliable support and stood up himself to join her as they moved slowly toward the door. The farewells, they both knew, would be lengthy and could not be rushed. As Alistair eased forward, pressing hands and accepting ebullient good wishes, Annabel Hillier appeared at his side. She was very flushed and slightly drunk. Wisps of light brown hair curled damply on her forehead. She stayed close to him as he rounded the corner into the corridor where the cold air from the front door came in with a chilling draught, making her shiver after the overheated atmosphere of the ballroom. Suddenly alone with her in the corridor, Alistair smiled benignly and said, 'You'll get cold. Go back inside.' He said it with avuncular firmness and she recognized it as a dismissal. But emboldened by more drink than she was accustomed to handle, she laid her hands on his chest and moved close enough to brush her body against him. His control weakened by drinking and fatigue, it was with considerable effort that he took her arms and gently removed them.

'Go back inside now,' he said tersely, 'like a good girl.' He had disengaged her just in time to be joined by the farewell committee who would see them out to their car. He helped Kate on with her coat and turned to say final goodbyes to the small throng gathering to see them off. To his relief, Annabel was now lost to view in the crowd.

Sliding into the car, he lowered the back of the passenger seat to a restful angle and kept his eyes closed for the journey home. It was half-past three before they got to bed and he was asleep almost instantly. The stimulation of Annabel's overture had triggered off enough frustration to produce vivid dreams of the woman who was really exciting him at the moment and he spent a restless night, waking to a headache and the depressing thought that his chances of succeeding with her might well be remote.

* * *

They had progressed from the soup to roast lamb when Tommy turned to Alistair, warmed by the relaxed intimacy of the lunch party and a fair amount of claret, 'You're doing the right thing, you know, old boy. We're all behind you up here.'

Alistair looked at him, taken aback by this sudden reference to something they had never even discussed. 'Just a toe in the water,' he murmured, repeating a disclaimer which was beginning to sound lame in his own ears. He saw Greville Lindsay grin, 'Don't be modest. We've all heard that you're being courted.'

'Have you?' Alistair asked with genuine surprise.

'It's the only way,' Tommy said seriously. 'Got to chat up the centre or we could get cut right out. And there are only a couple of you in the Government who can make it credible.'

Recovering from his shock, Alistair began to explore the topic. 'Rumour has it that the Labour front bench is hoping for deadlock for a while. They'd rather go into a coalition than have to govern on their own. It would give them some time in office to sort out their lunatic wing.' Anne Lindsay said, 'My God, that would be the worst of all possible outcomes.'

'Yes,' Tommy muttered, 'Labour gets a second wind, the Social Democrats get credibility and we get nothing.'

'The Social Democrats get credibility either way,' Alistair pointed out.

'Yes, but it does less damage if they come in with us,' Tommy rejoined.

'In fact,' Greville said, enunciating the statement with some enjoyment, 'it kills two birds with one stone – pulls our lot back to the centre and establishes the liberal lot as the real opposition in future and they're a hell of a lot less dangerous than the comrades.'

Dorothy Morton frowned and said with some exasperation, 'Surely it won't be as neat as that. The party in Parliament has been taken over by rightwingers who'd die before they'd go into a coalition. It won't wash.' Alistair smiled. He had always appreciated Dorothy's practicality. 'But you forget,' he told her, 'that in a close election a lot of those chaps will lose their seats. Most of them are in marginals. It will be the safe seats that will survive. There will be quite a few of us still around and rather fewer of them.'

Greville chortled, 'All those jumped-up unit trust salesmen will just have to hustle back to the City.'

'Don't know what the party thinks it's up to anyway,' Tommy was pursuing a favourite line. 'Been bloody lucky up to now with their confrontations but if we're not careful we'll have a general strike. The trouble is, they can't see it in London. They're not surrounded by it like we are up here.'

'And all in the name,' Greville mused obligingly, 'of some economic theory that you have to be a Jew to understand.'

Kate looked down the table at Alistair, 'But aren't you taking an awful risk? What if the Tories stay in? Won't they just see you as somebody who was prepared to do a bunk?'

He was touched by her concern but before he could reply, Tommy rushed in to reassure her. 'Don't worry, Kate. He's just establishing himself as a clever, pragmatic politican. No party can afford to dispense with people like that.'

'But he might not be trusted,' Dorothy put in, not wishing to alarm Kate but feeling obliged to state her warning.

'Nonsense,' Tommy insisted. 'Politics is a hard game. It's not boy scouts. No one expects you to do anything but play your own hand.'

They had moved on to the pudding before the subject was changed. Alistair was delighted by their enthusiasm if slightly alarmed by the degree of their knowledge. He had not realized how quickly gossip would travel. Unsure of what steps he could take to dampen speculation, he was left uneasily buoyed up by the approval. It was four o'clock before they drifted out to their cars. The Thurstons waved them off in the drive and then retreated back to the warmth of their drawing room.

Half an hour later Kate had gone to see to the dogs and Alistair found himself staring blankly into the fire, the ticking of the tall clock in the hall loud enough to be heard in the quiet room where he sat. There was something oppressive about this time of day on a Sunday. He could remember it from childhood, endless acres of unstructured time that seemed to hang in the air. He was suffering from the effects of inflicting too heavy a meal on to a digestive system already strained by the previous night's drinking, and this distress added to his fitful dissatisfaction. It was boredom that had always been his chief torment. He sometimes thought rather desperately that the pursuit of women and political ambition were the only antidotes to this frantic restlessness which always lay in wait to torture him. In the early stages of an infatuation, as he now was, it took the form of an obsessive sexual frustration which made everything unconnected to his chosen object infuriating in its irrelevance. But the focus of his preoccupation could change without warning to a professional goal or a short term political advantage. This mercurial intensity which flashed through his internal life was so much a feature of his character that it had never occurred to him to question it. When he was engrossed in one of his compulsions, he was elated and at one with himself, like a hound at the chase. When he was not, or when his pursuit was stalled or diverted, everything seemed to fall to pieces in his hands. He stood up and paced the room, unaware that this too was a characteristic habit when he was unbearably restive. Kate suddenly appeared in the room. He could not be sure how long she had been there. 'I've got to run over to Glaisdale,' she said. Glaisdale was where her parents had their estate. 'Don't suppose you want to come.'

'Rather not, really,' he admitted. She nodded and then looked at him. 'Are you all right?'

'Yes,' he said innocently, abashed that his state of mind was visible.

'What time do you want to get off tomorrow?' she asked.

'As early as I can. Before seven.'

'Thought you'd be impatient to get back,' she said wryly.

'Why?' he asked, honestly perplexed.

She said, 'I can always tell when you're on the verge of a conquest, Alistair. You look as if you're sitting on a hot brick.' She turned then and walked away, leaving him staring after her. He was not shocked so much by her knowing, or even by her sarcasm, but by the picture of himself she had conjured with a single sentence. She would know that to be thought immoral was just about acceptable to him, but to appear fatuous was not. He wondered at the degree of hostility that it must have taken to have dismissed him so flippantly. Deciding that he must lie down, he went upstairs to the small bedroom at the rear of the house. It was nearly dark as he stretched out on the bed, grateful to be left to cope with his indigestion and his ill-temper in solitude.

★ ★ ★

'That's your pretty blouse,' Emily said, stroking the sleeve. Priscilla smiled. 'Do you like it?' she asked, watching herself in the dressing table mirror as she put on her earrings. Instead of answering, Emily climbed on to the double bed and slid under the duvet. Priscilla turned round to face her. 'What are you doing?' she asked, laughing.

'Getting into your bed,' Emily replied with a challenging giggle.

'Doesn't Krista want you to be dressed when she gets back?'

Emily ignored this question, kicking her legs about happily in the big bed. Priscilla stood up and walked over to her. 'Come on,' she said, pulling the duvet away with playful suddenness, 'you've got to be ready to go.' Krista would be returning from delivering Jaimie to school, expecting to find Emily ready for playgroup. Looking down at her daughter still attired in a nightie, Priscilla realized that, in her preoccupation with her own preparations, she had not maintained her usual morning surveillance over Emily.

'Come on,' she said again, offering her hand this time. 'Let's find your clothes.' Emily jumped down from the bed and trotted along next to her. As they left the bedroom, Priscilla glanced at her own image in the wardrobe mirror. The recollection of how Thurston had watched her was no longer so fresh, but the fact that she was to meet him today produced flashes of recall which made her self-conscious. She could not stop seeing herself through his eyes. She realized that she was anxious about having to face him, especially alone over lunch. The lunch was a performance which she had not yet decided how to play.

* * *

It was Bertie Houghton who spotted Thurston as he approached the glass front door. Coming up to greet him from the rear of the gallery, Bertie smiled ingratiatingly, receiving him with the fulsome warmth of one who knew himself to be on terms of established intimacy. The old connection with Malvern which Bertie had nearly forgotten, was a link with Thurston which gave them the most indelible bond in British social life, which is to say that they numbered among their friends some of the same people. Alistair, functioning on the identical assumption, accepted Bertie's overtures with an informality which suited his desire to feel as familiarly relaxed in this gallery as he possibly could. As they walked back toward the office, Thurston could hear a female voice speaking in the declarative tone which people use for impersonal telephone calls. Bertie, a head shorter than Thurston, bobbed in front of him to open the office door. Priscilla was standing at the desk with her back to them, one knee resting on the seat of the desk chair as she spoke on the telephone. Hearing them enter, she turned and looked over her shoulder. Thurston smiled with instantaneous pleasure at the sight of her, using his effusion to conceal a tremor of nervousness. Returning his smile, she concluded her telephone call and then turned to face them. Always very aware of women's clothes, Thurston appraised the way her blue silk blouse enhanced the pink of her complexion. Silk was a fabric which seemed to cry out to be touched and he found himself wanting to take hold of her arm or run the palm of his hand along her back. The three of them stood chatting about Malvern, about Harold's reviews which had all been favourable, about the attendance for the show which had been exceptionally good. No one made reference to the Macmasters crisis, all of them maintaining by tacit agreement, the pleasant sociability of the occasion which would have been breached by raising the business concern which had brought them together. Bertie withdrew from them with civil diffidence as the small talk began to run out. Thurston turned to her then. Unconstrained by Bertie's presence, he could look her fully in the face with a directness which could only be assumed by two people alone together. She glanced up at him expectantly, taking the significance of his gaze to be a sign that he wished to say something to her. But he simply held her eyes for a moment and then said with casual warmth, 'I've booked a table at the Mayfair Hotel dining room. Shall we flag down a taxi or walk?'

The hotel was only a couple of blocks away and it was a bright, sunny day so she said that she would be happy to walk. She picked up her coat and handbag and they left the gallery together, Thurston at last finding an excuse to touch her arm as he guided her through the door. He had decided on this sumptuous, quiet dining room partly to flatter and impress her but as much, paradoxically, because it was very public and formal. It would have been a mistake to have lured her into some darkened, intimate restaurant at this stage. He would not have risked insulting her with such a presumption. She had been here once before on a social errand for an old public relations client and so the discreet architectural splendour and impeccably hushed service came as no surprise. Being with a member of the Government front bench did, nonetheless, add another dimension to the solicitudes which she was accorded. Thurston watched her accepting the deft obeisances which came to her as his companion, and knew that he was implicitly offering her this as part of his seduction. They were seated at a corner table, the management no doubt assuming that a Government minister would prefer not to be made conspicuous in the centre of a dining room. The pale grey walls with their baroque mirrors rose to a frieze where they met the high ceiling, studded at intervals with crystal chandeliers. In spite of the largeness and height of the room, its acoustics were muted. Deep carpeting and well-spaced tables provided a sense of privacy and comfortable ease. He asked her if she wanted a drink and she requested a Perrier. He ordered a whisky for himself, wanting to quieten his nerves which were unsettled to a degree that was threatening to undermine his confidence. She seemed more relaxed than he did and he could not decide whether this pleased him.

'Bertie was delighted that Malvern remembered him,' she said, her voice pleasant and open, her stage fright now having perversely vanished. He smiled. 'Unexpected stroke of luck. He never forgets a favour, Bevis. He's already recruiting his Private Secretary into the operation.'

She returned his smile and her warmth began to dissolve his tension. He could talk more readily now, with his usual fluency, about the gallery and how well Harold's pictures were selling. They were allies with a common goal and the conversation could emerge from the circumspections of mere acquaintance. He watched her as she talked, unaware of the fact that he was scarcely taking his eyes off her face and that his mood had changed. He was no longer at the stage of tentative calculation, but was now deeply and unselfconsciously engrossed in her, responding to every flicker of her facial expression as if his mind were an instrument that she was playing. As a consequence, his attentiveness to her was perfect because it was wholly sincere. There was no longer any need to anticipate or plan his reactions, his entire mental state being committed to understanding her every gesture. He had never realized that it was this capacity to lose himself in the desire to please a woman that made him so successful with them. His manner was invisible to him in his total absorption. There was as well, a sense of elation because he knew from experience that once he reached this point of obsession he always succeeded, the intensity of his compulsion never failing to carry him through. It sometimes seemed to him that this surge of confident resolve was the highest point of his sexual excitement.

She preferred not to have a heavy lunch and so they had only two courses and one bottle of young Beaujolais. The conversation had become lightly personal by the time they reached the coffee. She asked him when he had decided to go into politics and why, and they exchanged a smattering of information about their backgrounds and education. Nothing in anything that he said or did suggested impropriety. He was patient, feeling no need to press her, almost wanting to prolong this moment of secret certainty. As he glanced away to signal to the waiter for their bill, she looked at him, fully aware now of his intentions but unsure how seriously he intended to pursue them. Women who use their charm for professional purposes learn to deal carefully with masculine vanity. One rarely found oneself in an absolutely compromising situation, most men being content with sexual flattery and pleasant company. She wondered vaguely whether she might be out of her depth with this one. He turned back to her and caught her looking at him. A slight flush of pleasure raised the colouring of his face but his smile was gentle and unthreatening.

The influence of the wine was helping her to see how genuinely handsome he was. The greying dark hair which he wore long enough for it to curve around his ears, and very fair skin probably descended from some Celtic source. She suspected that he had been very thin as a younger man, still having the narrow, elongated frame that went with his height. But his body was starting to thicken, the midriff succumbing to middle age and the over-indulgence that went with political life. He was beginning to make regretful stirrings. It was necessary for him to be back at the House for Question Time that afternoon. She was quite happy to bring this encounter to a close, hoping that her attentions to him over lunch were going to count as sufficient payment for his help. As they emerged from the hotel into the hard winter sunshine, he accepted the offer of a taxi from the doorman and they slipped gratefully into the warmth of its back seat. It would drop her at the gallery before taking him on to Westminster. He did not sit unduly close to her in the taxi or make any move to touch her.

'I'll try to arrange for us to see Malvern with his Permanent Secretary by the end of the week,' he said, as they rounded the corner into Cork Street.

'I think Bertie had better come as well,' she said.

He nodded his assent as they pulled up in front of the gallery. The pavement was on his side and so he stepped out and held the taxi door open for her. Finally, as she stepped out on to the kerb, he allowed himself to put a hand briefly on her waist. 'I'll ring you as soon as I can arrange a date with him,' he said, taking leave of her. She smiled a goodbye and he hopped briskly back into the taxi. She watched it disappear around the corner before turning to go inside the gallery where Bertie would be waiting to hear how it had gone.

* * *

Thurston had attached a handwritten note to the printed invitation: 'It might be useful for you to come along and meet Malvern,' it read and it was signed, 'Alistair'.

'There'll be masses of people there,' Simon said despondently. 'I doubt that you'll get anywhere near him.'

Priscilla shrugged. 'I don't suppose it will do any harm to go.' It was a press reception for the opening of the Docklands Arts Complex, one of the schemes which the government regarded as a model of cooperation between state and private funding. Industrial sponsorship had initiated the project and the Ministry of Environment had matched it with subsidy from the Docklands Redevelopment Scheme. Thurston had been personally responsible for facilitating the plan through the Environment Ministry and it was his photograph which appeared on page two of *The Times* this morning, smiling triumphantly at the architect Nicholas Faverbridge whose adventurous design had engendered such controversy in the Press. Prince Charles, having expressed reservations about the proposed plans in the first instance had, it was reported, consented to perform the opening ceremony, thereby tacitly giving his approval to the final product. *The Times* quoted Thurston as saying that the Docklands Arts Centre, which was to house temporary exhibition space and a permanent modern collection (rumoured in *The Times* Arts Diary to consist largely of Tate Gallery overspill, 'the contents of the Tate's basement') as well as a museum of modern design, would 'take its place beside the Beaubourg in Paris as an international centre for modern art.'

The invitation to the press preview, prior to the official opening, came less than a week after Priscilla's lunch date with Thurston and two days after a telephone call from Alistair's private secretary to fix a date for her, Bertie and Thurston to meet the Permanent Secretary of the Arts Ministry. It would have seemed churlish not to go along to the reception even for what seemed the tenuous possibility of an introduction to the Arts Minister.

'You come as well,' Priscilla said to Simon, uncomfortable at the thought of attending alone.

'Don't think I can. Bertie's in New York next week. I'll have to be here late every night.' Simon put the invitation on her desk and turned to her. 'But you ought to go. He's obviously trying his best for us.'

Priscilla propped the invitation against the wall at the back of her desk and slipped Thurston's note into the top drawer. The press reception was five to seven p.m. She could get there easily after leaving the gallery on Tuesday night.

'Hi,' said an engagingly familiar voice behind her. She turned to see Debbie Ackerman standing in the office doorway.

'Hello,' Priscilla replied warmly. 'How are you?'

'I'm okay,' Debbie said brightly. Then she added significantly, 'I've just got back from Edinburgh.'

'Have you?' Priscilla asked. Debbie came to stand next to Priscilla's chair and leaned against her desk. 'It was great. It's a beautiful place.'

'Did you go on your own?' Priscilla asked. Debbie smirked with frank playfulness. 'No,' she said pointedly. Priscilla smiled as well, aware of what Debbie was telling her – that with Harold's neglect she had found other companionship. 'It was really nice,' Debbie went on, 'so *relaxed* and *un-intense.*' Then she gave Priscilla a look of candid female rapport and Priscilla smiled understandingly, genuinely pleased by Debbie's resilience. There was something almost imploringly intimate about Debbie's manner which made Priscilla respond in the only way that seemed appropriate, by matching her confiding, personal tone. 'I've just had an interesting invitation,' she said, pointing to the card standing on the back of her desk. Debbie glanced up at it obligingly. 'It's from that Minister who came to the opening,' Priscilla explained, falling in with the girlish camaraderie which Debbie offered.

'Oh, *really*?' Debbie asked, grinning with generous excitement at Priscilla's news. She picked up the card to look at it more closely. 'That could be very interesting,' she said, leaving

Priscilla unsure of whether she meant the reception or the fact of Thurston's overture.

'I haven't really decided whether to go or not,' Priscilla said finding it surprisingly easy to admit her mild anxiety to this girl who was a relative stranger but whose openness was so disarming.

'Oh, you've got to.' Debbie looked up with surprise. Her voice was cool and serious. 'These things are always worth going to. You can make contacts. Even if you don't actually meet people, you get seen and then people remember your face when they see you again.' The sudden calculating urgency of her tone took Priscilla by surprise. Debbie even looked older as she spoke these words, the ingenuous softness receding to reveal what Priscilla realized now was probably a woman of nearly thirty.

'Yes,' Priscilla replied, slightly startled, 'you're probably right.' Debbie was examining the card again. '*Everybody* will be at this,' she said earnestly. 'And if your friend the Minister invited you, you've got an excuse to go and find him. So you'll be seen with him and people will remember you for that.'

'Yes,' Priscilla said submissively. 'You're right.' Debbie grinned then and said, 'Good luck,' with cheerful envy.

'I'll tell you what,' Priscilla said. Debbie looked at her expectantly. 'Would you like to come with me? It's a bit daunting walking in to those things on your own.' Debbie's face was ecstatic with gratitude. 'You bet I would,' she exclaimed. Priscilla laughed good naturedly at Debbie's unaffected enthusiasm. She could not imagine any English person she knew having such an unguarded reaction and she realized that the prospect of Debbie's company at her next encounter with Thurston was rather reassuring.

* * *

They caught a taxi in Regent Street at five. Debbie had arranged to collect her at the gallery. 'That'll be plenty of time. You don't want to get there before six. Nobody does.' Priscilla had agreed and now at five-fifty the taxi was carrying them through the less salubrious parts of the East End toward the Dockland Arts Centre site.

'God,' Debbie said, looking out of her window. 'Is that it?' In what remained of the March daylight, a huge edifice loomed above the warehouse rooftops. The advance publicity had described it as an octahedron in shape with 'post-modernist allusions in the interior extensions from the planes constituting its basic structure.' One of the Sunday newspaper architecture correspondents had commented: 'For those whose solid geometry is shaky, an octahedron consists of two pyramids, one on top of the other and the bottom one upside down, so that the shape balances on a point. We can only hope that Faverbridge's building is as much a triumph of aesthetics as it will have to be of engineering.'

As they turned the final corner into the forecourt of the Arts Centre, it became apparent how the structural solution to Faverbridge's challenge had been resolved. The building's octahedral shape was constructed in a framework of bright blue steel girders, the top pyramid which they outlined consisting of tinted glass, the bottom one of yellow marble cladding on a network of blue and red steel. Supporting the sides of the lower pyramid were four steel staircases in red and blue which led to triangular doorways ('... the entrances, themselves triangular, reinforce both visually and structurally, the constructional principle of triangulation in which the unity of the design resides ...' read the press release). Running up through the centre of the structure was a transparent column which contained the lift shaft, the mechanism of which was visible at the apex of the upper pyramid, its cables in bright yellow 'forming a ribbon of incandescent colour which ascends the full height of the building.'

Priscilla and Debbie walked across the forecourt of blue and yellow concrete dotted with fountains on which red spotlights were focused so that they seemed to be spewing some strawberry flavoured soft drink. 'Shall we use the lift?' Priscilla asked, gazing doubtfully at the steep metal stairs which looked like festively coloured fire escapes.

'Oh, yes,' Debbie cried. 'The view will be fabulous.' They joined the small crowd at the bottom of the lower pyramid, whose base was a flattened point just large enough to take the square central column. Running alongside the glass tube which carried the lift was the exposed network of pipes and arteries which bore the building's essential services. The two women filed in their turn into the glass box, transparent even on its floor so that the ground could be watched falling away beneath as the lift shot up its full ten storey height. The ascent was greeted with gasps and shrieks of hilarity by the dozen occupants, pressed tightly against the almost invisible walls, while outside the coloured snakes of the services ran along like unwound intestine. As they arrived at the top, there was a burst of delighted applause. 'Isn't it *gorgeous*,' enthused one young man whose sleek black hair was cut very short at the back but hung in a long fringe across his forehead.

As they stepped out on to the yellow terrazzo marble floor, one wag behind Priscilla said, 'Pity he couldn't make the waste pipes transparent so that you could see the shit being carried out to the sewer.' It was the organizers' intention that the press audience, having reached the top of the building first, should then work their way down to the largest floor in the centre of the building. ('We'll put the bar in the middle. They'll be sure to find their way,' the publicity officer had said confidently.) As the floor on which they had emerged was tiny and served only as a vantage point for a splendid view of the river, it was obvious that they were intended to go down the open steel staircase which presented itself directly in front of them. As they descended in a giggling procession, they found themselves on a skeletal cat walk whose coloured girders guided them across the width of the top of the pyramid and into the first exhibition area which, with the use of a false ceiling hung from one triangular side, was concealed from the vast open space which they had traversed on the suspension bridge. ('The top exhibition space is a series of surprises as it opens up suddenly before one, hidden from view by turns in the central walkway.') This first area being empty, they continued to follow its curves around to where, through a triangular portal, the steel bridge resumed, this time marking a sharp downward diagonal across the widest point of the upper pyramid. 'Oooh,' someone called out in front, gripping the handrail as the stairs swooped dizzyingly down to their destination on the central floor.

'Isn't it *fantastic*?' Debbie said behind her. Priscilla nodded, clutching the rail more tenaciously as she saw that the floor on which they were arriving was glass, its transparency rendering both the steel girders which supported it and the floor beneath them, visible.

A knot of people had paused at the bottom, presumably to get their bearings in the huge space, but also to overcome their trepidation at having to traverse the disconcertingly invisible floor. Caught in the tailback on the stairs, Priscilla stood still and thus freed from concentration on her balance, was able to look round the vast central exhibition space which extended across the widest point of the octahedron. For this opening, the area was being used for a mixed show of the permanent art and design collection. The pictures hung on screens which were zig-zagged across the floor in diagonals. In the spaces between them were islands on which diverse objects stood in fetishized splendour. Between a wall of Stanley Spencer paintings and an array of Henry Moore drawings, there was a stand holding a bakelite radio in yellowed cream placed next to an upright vacuum cleaner of the type which Priscilla's mother had thrown out in the late 1950s. Some thirty feet away, an electric kettle stood with a matching stainless steel toaster, looking like the artfully composed detritus of the workmen's breakfast facilities. Just as the queue began to move down the ladder, the crowd at the bottom having dispersed itself gingerly across the floor, Priscilla caught sight of Thurston on the far side of the room, standing with his back to her in a circle of people. She glanced away immediately, surprised to discover how relieved she was that she had seen him before he had seen her. As her feet reached the floor, she too paused involuntarily finding the instinctive reluctance to walk on apparent nothingness inhibiting. It was necessary to fix one's eyes high enough to escape seeing the void below in order to break the paralysis. Just as she had begun to move off, Debbie seized her arm for support, giggling with delighted apprehension. Priscilla laughed as well and together they walked carefully at first but gaining in speed as they became more confident, across the room toward the long table which was serving as a bar. Glasses of red and white wine stood in rows along the table, while cheerful, pretty girls rushed around behind opening up more bottles as quickly as the glasses could disappear.

'Really *nasty* place to get drunk,' said a young man with bright red hair who stood near them peering downwards to the floor below. 'Makes you feel giddy when you're dead sober.' Debbie smiled at him in her gregarious way and said, 'What I don't understand is how they're going to be able to keep the floor clean enough. As soon as it gets dirty footprints on it the whole effect will be gone.'

The young man grinned. 'They'll just have to make everybody leave their shoes at the door like a Buddhist temple.'

Priscilla took a glass of white wine for herself and handed another one to Debbie who had become engrossed in the conversation with her new friend. As she turned to join them, she saw at the very edge of her vision, Thurston's figure turn in her direction. Although her sight of him had not been clear enough to be certain, she got the impression from a vague sense of increased intentness in his gaze, that he had seen her.

'I think it's an amazing experience,' the red-haired man was saying, 'but as a gallery it's very *intrusive*. I mean, how much attention can you pay to the exhibits when there's this amazing thing going on all around you.' Debbie nodded agreeably but replied, 'The novelty will probably wear off. It's like the Guggenheim in New York. Everybody was obsessed with the building at the beginning but after a while it settled down and now everybody looks at the pictures.' A tall thin girl with straggling black hair trotted up to them, 'Hi, Jason,' she exclaimed in pleased surprise to their red-haired companion.

'How are *you*?' he responded ecstatically. With this interruption, Debbie allowed her eyes to scan the room. 'Hey,' she said quietly to Priscilla, 'isn't that your friend over there?' Without looking to check, Priscilla knew that Debbie was indicating Thurston. She gave a very slight nod, more with her eyes than her head. Debbie grinned, recognizing Priscilla's girlish unease.

'Let's go over,' Debbie said mischievously. 'No,' Priscilla replied immediately, suddenly overcome with reluctance.

'Why not? He invited you.'

'He's with all the bigwigs at the moment,' Priscilla explained, rationalizing her own fit of shyness.

'All the better,' Debbie said. 'Come on.' She took hold of her arm with affectionate persuasiveness but Priscilla shook her head adamantly. Debbie sighed. 'Well,' she said, 'let's have a look at the show, then.' Still guiding Priscilla by the arm, Debbie led her towards the screen holding the Moore drawings, the route to which led them out into a more thinly populated stretch of the floor. As they walked across the open area, Priscilla was aware of her visibility and she averted her eyes carefully from Thurston's direction, almost enjoying her own determination to play hard to get.

They stopped in front of Henry Moore's wartime drawings of the underground and as Priscilla gazed at the familiar rows of prone figures, she heard Debbie say thoughtfully, 'It's odd, looking at those drawings in this place.'

'What do you mean?' Priscilla asked.

'Well, they're all about being confined in this claustrophobic space, and here we are in this huge, transparent building. It's almost as if the drawings were mocking – some kind of grim reminder.'

Priscilla looked at her in surprise not only because it was a remark she would not have expected from Debbie but because it was a thought she could not imagine having had herself. It never occurred to her to see art objects as making any comment on their settings. She had watched a Modigliani portrait sold for a fortune in a sumptuous London saleroom the previous year without reflecting on the irony of that painter's life and death in a Parisian garret. Art works were a movable feast, to be displayed wherever they found themselves – homeless, transportable, consumable. It seemed no more or less appropriate to her to see a Russian icon in a Bond Street gallery than a van Gogh. Struck by Debbie's observation, she wanted to reply to it. While she searched for words, she noticed Debbie looking expectantly past her head and, a second later, felt a hand touch her elbow.

'Hello,' Alistair said and in the instant that it took to recognize his voice, she had turned round to see him standing behind her. He was smiling in his engaging way but his eyes held a familiarity which made the professional warmth less impersonal. She said hello and immediately introduced him to Debbie who responded, to Priscilla's relief, with discreet politeness.

'What do you think of it?' Thurston asked, casting a look round the gallery.

'A bit overwhelming,' Priscilla replied. He smiled wryly. 'It's going to attract a lot of controversy, that's for sure.'

'Most of the comments I've heard have been favourable,' Priscilla volunteered helpfully.

'Really?' he said. 'Well, we shall just have to see what the papers say later in the week. Even if they attack it, there'll be a lively debate and it will draw the crowds.'

'A lot of people hated the Pompidou Centre, at first,' Debbie put in.

'Yes,' Thurston agreed, 'that's right, and now it's reckoned to be a great success.' Glancing back over his shoulder, he said to both of them, 'Come and meet some people.' Debbie maintained a tactful distance when he fell into step with Priscilla as they walked toward a circle of people whose self-contained animation marked them out unmistakably as the most important group at the gathering. The outer perimeter of this circle gave way as Alistair approached, allowing him and the two women in his company to enter, curious attention immediately focusing on his female companions. In the centre of this assembly stood a rather fleshy young man with curly hair and yellow framed glasses. 'I don't want it to be just another collection of *objects*', he was saying feelingly. 'It has to plug into the whole dynamic of social aesthetics which is about popular taste. That's the thing about consumer products, isn't it – that they're direct expressions of popular culture and if this place is to work, it's got to be about the world in which design *happens*.'

Priscilla recognized the man holding forth as Jasper Lejeune, the director of the Centre's design collection. In the rapt audience surrounding him were a number of familiar faces whom Priscilla was vaguely attempting to identify when Alistair took her elbow and pointed her in the direction of the Arts Minister. Malvern beamed with effusive graciousness as he shook hands.

The two men stood on either side of her, separating her from Debbie.

'Priscilla says that people seem to like the place,' Alistair said, his words addressed to Malvern but his eyes still on her face.

'Oh, good,' Malvern boomed at her with exaggerated relief. 'It would be splendid if it could be a great success.'

Priscilla, slightly overwhelmed by his bombastic attention, replied, 'Oh, I'm sure it will.' She was able to see past Thurston, and noticed before he did, the approach of a man who accosted Alistair from behind with jovial recognition. Turning abruptly to face Harry Fitzjohn, Alistair smiled and Priscilla drew back self-effacingly as they greeted each other. Seeing her start to move away, Alistair seized her arm. 'This is Priscilla Burford,' he said to Fitzjohn, pronouncing her name with affectionate significance.

'Hello,' Fitzjohn said, gazing at her with such frankly delighted appraisal that for a moment it seemed as if he might congratulate Thurston on the acquisition of her. Standing between Malvern and Thurston, he closed the gap in the semicircle of men around her so that her view of Lejeune, Debbie and the rest of the party was lost.

'Priscilla handles all the publicity for the Houghton Gallery,' Alistair announced. Teasing her proprietorially, he added, 'She can tell you all about the virtues of Harold Lewis's paintings.'

'Aah,' Malvern said with avuncular condescension. 'They are rather good, aren't they. But I understand that the recent ones are very different.'

'Yes,' she said diffidently. 'They have changed quite a lot.'

'Much bolder and splashier, I've heard.' She nodded agreement. He leaned toward her with indulgent interest. 'What do you think of them? Is he on the right track?'

Slightly flustered by this, Priscilla hesitated. Fitzjohn smiled broadly and said, 'Now, now Bevis. You're putting her on the spot.' Alistair broke in, 'She does approve of the new paintings. She told me all sorts of convincing things about them at his opening.' They all smiled down at her and she felt herself flinch before the force of their predatory attentiveness. Perhaps sensing her discomfiture, Alistair said more gently, 'Have you met Jasper?' She shook her head, dumbstruck by reticence. He-motioned to her to come with him and as they moved toward Lejeune, Priscilla caught sight once again of Debbie who was talking happily to a young man with an earring and cropped hair. Relieved to be reunited with her, Priscilla smiled in a way which Debbie, with her peculiar perceptiveness, recognized as an invitation to rejoin them. Harry Fitzjohn, who had accompanied them in Lejeune's direction, looked up inquisitively as Debbie arrived at Priscilla's side. Noticing his interest, Debbie paused expectantly so that Priscilla could introduce them. On hearing his name, Debbie broke into her most radiant smile. 'I've got a friend who works for you on the *Daily News*,' she said.

'Have you?' he asked delightedly. 'Who's that?'

'Frank Willis – he's a photographer. We've done some work together.'

'Oh Frank, of course. He's one of our best photographers.' Fitzjohn grinned expansively. 'What have you worked on with him? Are you a model?'

Debbie made a jokingly reproachful face, taking him to task for his assumption that any good looking girl must serve a decorative function. 'No,' she said pointedly. 'I'm a journalist.' He touched her arm and said, 'I am sorry,' with good humoured self-parody, 'but do take it as a compliment.' She gave a laugh which from any English woman would have sounded coy, and answered, 'All right, I will.'

Thurston, by that time, was leading Priscilla away toward Lejeune who was carrying on his ebullient oration for the benefit of a small knot of people at one end of the bar. As they approached, he was saying, 'I just don't think I'll have *time* to do another series. Thames and Hudson are pestering me for the book and this place is going to need all my attention for the next year.'

Seeing Thurston approach, Lejeune turned to him with immediate deference. 'It's getting off to a good start,' he said to Alistair with ingratiating enthusiasm.

'Yes, I think it is,' Alistair replied kindly. Then he turned to Priscilla. 'Have you met Jasper?' he asked rhetorically, then to Lejeune, 'This is Priscilla Burford from the Houghton Gallery.'

'Hi,' Lejeune said quickly, barely glancing at her. He turned to Thurston. 'The New York visitation are already talking about touring exhibitions. They loved the idea of the cigarette posters.'

'Excellent,' Thurston said.

'I really think,' Lejeune went on earnestly, 'that it's that kind of international connection that we need. British design can be so *parochial.*'

Thurston was beginning to show the same signs of restiveness that he had toward the end of their lunch date. Accustomed to the behaviour of men under professional pressure, Priscilla glanced at him with sympathetic understanding while Lejeune's monologue continued. When Jasper paused for breath, she turned to Alistair and asked, 'Do you have to go?' Her tone was so discreetly solicitous that it made him start with pleased surprise.

'I'm afraid so,' he answered gently, speaking quietly enough to make it clear that the communication of regret was intended only for her. 'The car is waiting to take me back to the House,' he went on with almost domestic familiarity. 'Can we drop you somewhere in the West End?'

Slightly taken aback, she replied, 'Oh, that's very kind.' Looking round the huge room quickly, she said, 'I came with Debbie. I'll have to find out how she's getting back.'

'We can take her as well,' he offered magnanimously and began looking round himself, to locate her. 'Aah,' he said after a moment. 'I believe she's still firmly in Harry's grip.'

Priscilla turned to look in the direction of Thurston's gaze. Debbie was standing in her artlessly elegant way, listening responsively to Harry Fitzjohn who loomed genially over her, seeming to use his large body to screen her from the rest of the room. Priscilla said that she would see if Debbie was ready to leave and moved off in their direction with Thurston following a few paces behind. Debbie noticed her as she approached and gave her an ecstatic smile.

'We've been offered a lift back,' Priscilla said. Harry boomed out cheerfully, 'She doesn't need a lift. She's coming to dinner with me.' Priscilla looked quickly at Debbie whose face had the inscrutable serenity which Priscilla had first seen at Harold's private view. Priscilla continued to look at her for a few seconds wanting to determine whether this arrangement was really something to which Debbie had agreed. Sensing her anxiety, Debbie smiled again and said sweetly but with unmistakable finality to the offer of a lift, 'Thanks, anyway.'

Left feeling slightly awkward, Priscilla murmured a goodbye.

'I'll come in to the gallery to see you,' Debbie called after her, her voice taking on a reassuring tone as if it were Priscilla who was putting herself at risk. Thurston asked when Priscilla reached him, 'Does she have other plans?'

'It would seem so,' she answered, mildly astonished at Debbie's readiness to go off with a man who manifested so clearly the overbearing lasciviousness of middle age. Thurston led her toward the lift and with a half dozen other people they were dropped down the transparent chute to ground level.

'The car should be back here,' Thurston said, guiding her with a touch of his hand on her back. The driver hopped out of the front seat as soon as he spotted the Minister making his way through the crowd. He held the official car's back door open and Thurston handed Priscilla in before him, then slipped in beside her. 'Where would you like to be delivered?' he asked with a consideration that stopped just short of tenderness.

'Any tube station will do,' she answered hurriedly.

'Where do you have to end up?'

'Highgate.'

'Then you want the Northern Line, don't you?' As the driver started the engine, Thurston leaned forward and said, 'We want to drop the lady at Embankment tube, John.' The driver made an obedient noise and they pulled away slowly through the excited crowd of people who milled about the forecourt. Alistair leaned back against the seat. Its generous width allowed them to sit a comfortable distance apart but she still found herself closer to him than she had ever been before. When she turned and caught his profile in the irregular light, she could see the texture of his skin and the curve of an incipient double chin softening the jaw. His hand rested, palm down, on the seat between them, unthreatening and still, but there was, even so, a sensation which ran through her thigh as if the spirit of the hand were reaching out of itself to touch her. He turned to her then and said, 'You look very pensive. What's the matter?' It was said lightly enough not to be offensively personal but he knew instantly from her withdrawal that he had overstepped the mark. Torn between the desire to sulk at her reserve, and eagerness to repair the damage, he was silent for a moment. Then fortuitously, they turned a corner which brought the gallery back into distant view through her side window. He pointed to it and smiled. 'Extraordinary sight, isn't it?' She turned to look. 'Remarkable,' she agreed. They were able then to resume civilities. She asked pleasingly curious questions about the Arts Complex and he gave her an entertaining account of the negotiations which had preceded its development. By the time they reached Embankment tube station, he knew that she was enjoying his company and that it was not, as he would have found unendurable, a relief to her to get out of the car. They pulled up and the driver was out of his seat to open her door in a deftly instantaneous movement. Thurston wished her good night with an unambiguous friendliness which was so bland that she was almost disappointed.

* * *

Harry Fitzjohn became a rather different man once he and Debbie were alone together. The ebullient buffoonery of his public advances gave way to a firm, almost paternal protectiveness. In the gallery, he had strutted and performed, flattering her with an extravagant monopoly of her attention. Having her to himself, convinced in his experience of women that she was impressed by him, his voice dropped to a muted gentlemanliness and the mature, sexually confident man that he was, emerged. They had dinner in a quiet Mayfair restaurant. He asked her about herself, her education, her childhood in America.

'Are you completely alone in this country?' he asked at one point, with real concern. She seemed surprised at the question. 'I've made lots of friends here.'

'Well yes,' he said dismissively, 'but you have no roots here, no family.' His alarm over this struck her as touching but she simply shrugged as if it were not an issue for her. Then she smiled at him, looking directly into his eyes. 'Do you think I need looking after?' Her gaze held him transfixed and for a few seconds he could not find his voice. 'Yes, I certainly do,' he replied hoarsely. Debbie, aware that his attraction was becoming something more urgent, made a point of touching him on occasion throughout the remainder of the meal wanting to test his composure which remained impeccable, perhaps because he was aware that her provocation was a game in which he must not lose face.

She got back into his car after they left the restaurant without questioning their destination. Before starting the engine, he turned and looked at her for a moment as if he wanted to eat her, but he did not touch her. Reduced nearly to distraction by her flirtation, he said with an enforced self-control which sounded peremptory, 'Are you coming home with me?'

'If you want me to,' she answered, as if she thought he was angry with her. His face softened then and he said very quietly, 'Yes, I want you to.'

His London flat was in a mansion block near Maida Vale. They took the tiny lift up to the third floor and he let her in, turning on the light switch to illuminate a sumptuously furnished set of rooms, decorated in the cool, impersonal style of a company *pied-à-terre*. He brought her into the living room and her eye was immediately caught by the vivid colouring of a lithograph on the white wall. 'That's a Paolozzi,' she said.

'Yes, that's right,' he agreed pleasantly. 'Would you like a brandy?'

She shook her head and continued to look up at the print with genuine interest. 'I've always loved that series of his. They've got an almost oriental sense of design.' He came and stood behind her, glancing at the picture curiously, murmuring agreement. Then he put his hand on her waist and said, 'Come and sit down.' She turned to him and knew from his face that he would tolerate no further teasing. Smiling, she reached up and put her arms around his neck. Nearly done in by this sudden gesture, he looked down at her rapturously as if he could not believe his luck and whispered, 'What a sweet girl you are.' He kissed her then with the unfaltering, proficient eroticism of an older man and, with that, immediately reclaimed control of their encounter.

Part Two

PRISCILLA SAW WITH relief that the front of the house was dark. If Julian had been back, the living room lights would have been on and the curtains drawn. Julian disliked getting home and not finding her there so she had nearly run from Highgate tube station. She had managed to reach home before him even though it was nearly half-past six. Krista would be downstairs in the kitchen with Emily and Jaimie. As her key released the mortice look on the door, she could hear Emily's voice shrieking with laughter from the basement, and she was doubly relieved. This last bout of tonsillitis had laid Emily so low that even the usually miraculous antibiotics had been slow to act. The unmistakable sound of her return to good spirits made Priscilla smile with delight even before she was fully into the house. They were sitting on the wicker sofa, Krista and the two children, at the garden end of the big basement kitchen. Emily, still in her invalid's pyjamas and dressing gown, had been so engrossed in her own laughter at the Dr Seuss book which Krista was reading that she had failed to hear Priscilla on the stairs. Now she looked up in ecstatic surprise, squealed with happiness and ran to her mother. Still just light enough at four to be lifted, she put her arms around Priscilla's neck and leapt gleefully into her arms. Her face felt mercifully cool after the fever of the past week and Priscilla kissed both her cheeks with pleasure. Jaimie, more aloof in his seven-year-old dignity, remained on the sofa but smiled blissfully when Priscilla walked to him, still carrying Emily, and smoothed her hand over his blond head.

'We had fish fingers for supper!' Emily was reporting excitedly as she was sat down on the sofa. Krista rose to let Priscilla take her place between the two children. 'Did you?' Priscilla asked. Then she turned to Jaimie who sat beside her, scuffing the toes of his shoes aimlessly against the quarry tiled floor. 'How was school?' she asked.

'Okay,' he said, as he always did.

'Did you read in assembly?'

He nodded with quiet pride, then said, 'Miss Robertson said I was the best because she could hear me all the way at the back of the hall.'

Priscilla smiled at him and he beamed with righteous satisfaction at her approval. Emily was climbing on to her lap, 'I made a picture today with my fingerpaints,' she burbled, pressing her face close to Priscilla's.

'Really? Can I see it?

'Krista put it on the radiator in my room to dry.'

'Oh, that's good. I'll have a look when I go upstairs.'

Krista, who was peeling potatoes at the sink, smiled at them and said, 'The paint was a bit thick so it might take a while to be dry.'

They all heard Julian's key in the door and Jaimie hopped to his feet in excited anticipation. Priscilla disengaged herself from Emily to walk to the bottom of the stairs. As he came down, she was standing there to greet him as she knew he would want her to be. He smiled at her as he came into the room and handed her a wrapped bottle of wine.

'What's this?' she asked.

'Oddbins had it on sale. Too good to resist.'

She unwrapped the bottle of Beaune and put it on the work surface. Emily was clamouring at Julian's side, pulling on his hand. Priscilla led her protesting back to the sofa, murmuring that she should let Daddy relax for a minute. Julian was uncorking the wine now with Jaimie hovering at his elbow. Priscilla took the meat out of the fridge and fell into their routine of meal preparation with Krista.

* * *

It was eight by the time they sat down to eat together, the children in bed, Krista gone to her English evening class.

'How was Geoffrey?' she asked, enquiring about his most difficult encounter of the day.

'As boring as ever. At least he paid for lunch this time.'

'Did you have to see him alone?

'No, thank God. William came. He did most of the talking. I think we've won him round but he's such a bloody minded sod, he won't admit it.'

He sipped some of the wine, 'Not bad, is it?' Without waiting for her reply, he went on, 'By the way, the Belgian contingent are coming next week. We'll have to do our share of the entertaining.'

Oh God, she thought but she said nothing only looking at him with faint protestation. He carried on, 'They arrive on Monday so we'll have to make it dinner on Thursday.'

This was more than she could bear. Julian knew that Thursday was the worst possible day for her since it was the evening that the gallery stayed open until seven and they liked her to be there.

'Must it be?' she asked plaintively.

Primed for her objection, he became instantly irascible. 'Yes, it must. They go back on Friday and the other evenings are tied up with meetings.'

She had a thought. 'Couldn't we take them out for a meal? I could meet you in town after the gallery shuts.'

'Oh, for God's sake, Priscilla,' he exploded in exasperation. 'They'll be eating every meal in restaurants and hotels while they're here. They need to be invited to a home. It's only civil. I'm always taken to someone's home for dinner when I'm over there. It isn't that much to ask.' The bitterness of his outburst arose, like the excessive antagonism of many apparently trivial disagreements in a marriage, from the fact that there was a history of such disputes. The need to entertain his business contacts often conflicted with her professional life. While he accepted, and even took pride in, her career, it could not seriously be considered as a competitor to the priorities dictated by his own ambition. He subsided into silence then and Priscilla knew that even acquiescence would not now save her from an evening of sullen recrimination. Her raising of an objection was sufficient to arouse his anger and she kicked herself mentally for having protested. He was furious with her for not *wanting* to do this for him. To state in her own defence that she could not help her inclinations and that, more often than not, she did forgo them in his interests, would have been pointless. He had never articulated to himself the source of this kind of anger, perhaps because if he had it would have seemed too patently outrageous, and because it was unstated, it was not susceptible to argument. He would simply nurse his sense of betrayal until time and her actions restored his good temper.

They were still sitting in silence over the last of the wine when Krista returned from her class. Her arrival required a resumption of pleasantries and good manners which they both accepted thankfully. As Krista retired to her room with a cheerful goodnight, Julian proffered the bottle to offer Priscilla the last of the wine but she said that he could have it, and with that they fell into conversation without reference to the two hours which had just passed.

* * *

'The silly old fart. I really thought we had it.' Bertie had slammed the telephone down on to the desk so hard that she feared for its thin plastic shell. His anger came out in hot, vituperative eruptions while Simon, panicky himself over the gallery's future, made empty soothing noises. Priscilla's own disappointment left her speechless. After all their careful negotiation, all their tact, Macmasters had, at the last moment, mercurially decided to pull out of the plan. It was not clear whether he had simply grown impatient with the tedium of the process, felt that insufficient sycophantic attention was being paid to his own importance or whether, in fact, he had suspected that the arrangement was in other people's interests more than his own. A terse letter from one of his aides was followed by a futile telephone conversation which confirmed that Macmasters had lost interest. Priscilla was most appalled by the prospect of having to inform the Ministry. Thurston had gone to such trouble, arranging for them to meet with officials from the Arts Ministry, and his own department, offering support and advice at every stage. It would be agonizingly embarrassing to have to announce the complete collapse of the venture without even being able to offer an adequate explanation. She had brooded over the breakfast table, knowing that as chief go-between, it would be her responsibility to break the news to Thurston.

'Don't be silly,' Julian had muttered dismissively. 'He won't give a damn. Things fall through all the time. Dealing with rich people who run on whims, it has to be expected. Thurston will have more important things on his mind.'

She was inordinately hurt and offended by this, not by Julian's manner, which was his habitual one at this hour, but by the suggestion that the project and therefore that she, would be of little account to Alistair Thurston. Julian's words, uttered with such matter of fact confidence, struck her immediately as obviously true. Of course, this would hardly have been a ripple on the surface of Thurston's busy life – a diverting foray into art world politics, an opportunity to socialize, to show off, perhaps, to an attractive woman. He was, as she had said herself, a professional charmer. Their meetings had not subverted his thoughts, invaded his imaginings as they had hers. She went quiet then and remained so through the morning at the gallery.

'Somebody,' Simon was saying ominously, 'is going to have to tell the Ministry people.'

She nodded. 'I'll do it,' she said resignedly. Simon smiled at her with melancholy gratitude. Bertie was buried too deep in his outrage to acknowledge her offer. Swallowing her reluctance, she turned on her revolving chair to pick up the telephone and dial Thurston's private Ministry line, the number of which she knew by heart. His Principal Private Secretary answered. She knew his face well, pictured him as he spoke. He greeted her with pleased recognition when she gave her name. In a fit of cowardice she did not simply leave a message asking Thurston to ring her which would have involved giving him the news directly but instead, told it to the Secretary.

'Would you tell the Minister,' she said with painful clarity, 'that we are terribly sorry but Mr Macmasters has decided to withdraw the proposal to offer his collection. Please give him our deepest apologies for wasting his time and say that we are very grateful for all the help he has offered.'

The Secretary accepted the message with a gracious murmur, his tone kindly in response to her obvious mortification. Then she rang off, feeling with complete conviction that that was the last she would hear of the matter and of him.

'Well,' Simon said, sighing deeply, 'you win some, you lose some.'

'Stupid arsehole,' Bertie muttered implacably meaning – they all knew – Macmasters and not Simon.

It was two hours later that Simon came to call her from the basement where she was putting away some prints. 'Telephone call for you from the Ministry,' he breathed. She went to the telephone, discomfited by her own hopefulness that it might be Thurston himself.

'Priscilla Burford,' she said into the receiver.

'Priscilla,' he began, his voice warm with concern, 'what's happened?'

'God knows,' Priscilla confided despairingly, overwhelmed by gratitude at his gentleness. 'He's just gone off the idea for some inexplicable reason. And we were so close to working it out.'

She heard him sigh with exasperation. 'I wonder what he's up to. Have you met with him?'

'No, we just had a note from one of his staff yesterday. When Bertie rang this morning, Macmasters' secretary was evasive and unhelpful.'

Thurston was quiet for a few seconds. Then he asked, 'How late will you and Bertie be at the gallery?'

She was a bit taken aback. 'Well, we close at five but we could stay on later.'

'If I can get to you by about half-past five, would that be all right? I think we should have a chat.'

Of course that would be all right, she replied quickly. When she rang off, she rushed delightedly out of the office to find Bertie and tell him that perhaps all was not lost. Then she rang home to tell the au pair that she was going to be late, to prepare the food for dinner, and that she would probably be home by half-past seven.

It was just after six when Alistair rang the gallery's front door bell. He came in with a flood of apologies for his lateness – it had been impossible to leave a meeting which had run on. Bertie brushed aside his effusions with grateful cordiality and offered him a drink. Sitting down with his whisky on the office sofa, he looked across at Priscilla who had turned her chair to face him. Giving her a tired smile, he said, 'You're looking a bit distraught.'

She smiled in some embarrassment, made shy by his perceptiveness. 'It's all so shambolic,' she said, 'and mystifying.'

'I'm not sure,' he said importantly.

'What do you mean?' Bertie blurted. It had not occurred to him that Thurston might have information which was not available to him.

'I think,' Thurston said with frank confidentiality, 'that what the old dear really wants is a gong.' He crossed his legs and leaned back, completely at ease. There was something about the half-darkened gallery, the privacy of their conversation or perhaps the urgency of the crisis which was making him relax into worldly irreverance. He had never spoken so cynically to them before. His indiscretion was a compliment to their friendship.

'So why drop out now?' Priscilla asked, her voice too dropping any falsity.

'He was snubbed last week by Number Ten. A reception for the sort of chaps who give lots of money to the party. He expected to be asked and wasn't.' Thurston raised his eyebrows in a parody of humiliation. 'Probably thinks that if he's that far out of the inner circle, he's not likely to get anything no matter how many paintings he throws to the nation.'

'Christ.' Bertie was dumbfounded. He saw the future of his gallery sliding into oblivion on grounds over which he had no influence whatever. Priscilla too had subsided into dejection.

Thurston said then, 'It's not unsalvageable, I don't think.' He enjoyed the brightening of Priscilla's eyes. 'I've had a little word with the Chancellor's PPS. They're having a dinner next month for businessmen who've made notable contributions to the economic recovery. Macmasters isn't quite big enough commercially to be in that league but I've got the Chancellor's office to invite him.' He smiled at Priscilla's unguarded delight. 'Can't promise miracles ...' he murmured with mild self-deprecation.

'But he's already said he's pulling out,' Priscilla objected. 'Can he just do a volte-face?'

'We'll write him a *very* nice letter,' Bertie said quickly, already composing it in his head. 'Understand your hesitation ... perfectly prepared to consider other forms of arrangement ... would he like to discuss his objections ...'

'Time the letter to arrive next week,' Thurston put in. 'That's when he'll get the invite.' They all laughed with collusive enjoyment.

'Will the old boy get a handle to his name, then?' Bertie asked, taking up Thurston's invigorating tone.

Alistair shrugged. 'Not for me to say. It will depend on how many there are ahead of him in the queue.' He drank the last of his whisky and Bertie rushed over to refill his glass. He topped up Priscilla's as well. The whisky and her elation over Thurston's visit were making her light-headed. She watched Alistair sip his drink and when he met her eyes she did not look away. They were settling now into jocular camaraderie, their relations oiled by shared duplicity and common purpose. Thurston started to talk of other things, holding forth entertainingly on the foibles of one of his well-known colleagues as he recounted his insider's knowledge of a recent government fiasco. His eye strayed to a French drawing leaning against the wall.

'Isn't that lovely?' he said, clearly taken by the pastel nude.

'It is rather nice, isn't it?' Bertie agreed proudly. 'I've just bought a collection of them. We're sorting through them now to see if they'll make a show.'

'It's wonderful,' Thurston said seriously. He had become, for a moment, the intent aesthete she had first met at the private view. She realized that she was watching the changes in his facial expressions with fascination, could hardly take her eyes off him. Suddenly he became alert, aware of the time. She was almost relieved that this meant he would be leaving, freeing her from this entranced paralysis. But instead he said, glancing at them both with charming impulsiveness, 'Are you doing anything for dinner?' Bertie looked delighted. 'I'm not, no,' he said and looked expectantly at Priscilla. She blinked in surprise. About to say that she really had to get home, she heard in anticipation how ungrateful and mean spirited it sounded. Julian was in Birmingham and would not be home until nearly midnight which, in some respects made things easier but also meant that the children would see neither of them that evening.

'Do come,' Alistair said keenly. 'We'll just have a quick meal somewhere close by.'

'All right,' she said as if persuaded, knowing that this answer had been inevitable all along. The slight haze of the whisky seemed to merge in her head with the sensations she felt when he looked at her. Her inhibitions had lapsed and she was giving in to the narcissistic pleasure of being desired.

'I'll have to phone my constituency secretary before she leaves,' Thurston said, now businesslike once again. He walked over to the desk where Priscilla sat and reached for the telephone beside her. As he stood next to her chair, she watched his fingers dialling, noticed the fraction of striped shirt cuff which extended beyond his jacket sleeve. When he began to speak, her eyes lifted to his face which was composed now in official preoccupation. He exchanged a few tersely efficient remarks with the secretary on the other end of the phone, then asked her to transfer him to the Whips' office. While he waited to be connected he glanced down at Priscilla's face which was turned upwards to him and winked at her with avuncular indulgence. Then he was put through and once again, his concentration returned to the telephone.

When he had finished, Priscilla said, 'I'll have to ring, as well.' With some self-consciousness, she rang her own home and heard herself say, 'Krista, it's me. I'm afraid I'm not going to get home for supper. Could you eat with the children and tell them I'll come up to see them when I get in later.' This last statement, she knew, was pointless. They would be long asleep before she got home.

They went to a cheerful Italian restaurant in Soho which was noisy and gregarious enough to break through Priscilla's hypnotic mood. The atmosphere of the meal was one of exuberant good humour. Bertie was in good form, amusing them both with his outrageous anecdotes and camp mimicry. They got through two bottles of wine between the three of them and although Priscilla drank quite a lot of it, she felt less drunk than she had in the office when she had had whisky on an empty stomach. She felt euphoric now but clearheaded. Alistair had become a source of trustworthy delivering strength. He had ushered them into the restaurant, having a word with the headwaiter which made it unnecessary for them to have booked. They were seated at a round table in a corner. The Italian waiters teased her with their harmless lasciviousness while Alistair looked on in benign, proprietorial pleasure. As far as she could recall, he had not touched her at all during the evening except once in a casual way, just a hand on her arm. But he held her eyes as they talked and his smile made her feel as though she were being caressed. They were there for two and a half hours, their conversation largely gossip although there was the occasional excursion into some serious issue of art or politics. Afterwards Alistair and Bertie both walked her to Leicester Square tube station where she took the Northern Line back to Highgate, grateful that she had not brought the car that day since she was in no fit state to drive.

It was half-past eleven when she got home. Julian was not back yet and the house was quiet. She looked in on the sleeping children and then undressed quickly not wanting to be up when Julian returned, climbing into bed without even brushing her teeth. The bed seemed to float under her and she realized before falling asleep that she was actually quite drunk.

The next thing of which she was aware was Julian saying testily, 'You had a restless night.' It was early morning, too early even for the alarm clock to have gone off but she was obviously, she realized, awake. Taking in his words, she had an impression of a night full of dreams the details of which she could not remember but which left her breathlessly uneasy. When she had opened her eyes fully, she found that the sense of revulsion was not only in her mind. Her stomach was turning over and the taste in her mouth reminded her of what she had eaten and drunk the night before. A small, involuntary moan escaped from her.

'What's the matter?' Julian asked, only half awake himself.

She pulled herself into more alertness. 'Nothing,' she said. Then, realizing that she could not hope to conceal how she felt, she added, 'Just an upset tummy. Must have eaten something ...'

He turned over to face her, laying a hand on her belly. 'You're not pregnant, are you?' He asked it with a hint of cheerful hopefulness. It had always been clear that he had quite liked her pregnancies, finding them reassuring, enjoying the docility that they induced. She shook her head mutely and dragged herself out of bed.

Memories of the previous evening came back with varying degrees of distinctness as she got through the morning routine fighting fatigue and bouts of nausea. Jaimie asked piercingly why she had not been home for dinner and she replied, for Julian's benefit, that the gallery had had to entertain someone and she had got roped into it. The half truth came easily especially as it was consistent with her physical state. 'Where did you take them,' Julian joked, 'an oyster bar?' When the au pair had taken Jaimie to school and Julian had gone to the office, she had only to contend with Emily's preparations for playgroup. She felt like Alice in Wonderland waking under the tree to find that everything which had so excited and threatened her had vanished. Her state of mind the previous evening, especially in its early phase at the gallery, appalled her in recollection. The whole episode took on an unreal distance and she could almost believe that it had happened years before, to herself at quite a different stage of life.

* * *

Julian was knotting his tie as Priscilla folded the last two shirts into his suitcase. He always wanted her to pack for him since she had learned the skill, in her much travelled early publicity career, of packing clothes in such a way that they would not crease. His hair was still damp from the shower and she worried that he would be venturing out into the cold with wet hair. 'Doesn't matter,' he murmured absently to her admonitions. 'It'll dry in the taxi.'

Julian's business trips abroad were a frequent enough ritual for them to have the preparations well-rehearsed. He was going to Bonn this time and she had just managed to get some German currency for him this afternoon. She put his passport in the outer pocket of his hand luggage where he always carried it, with half of the travellers' cheques. The remaining cheques went into the suitcase so that he would not be caught out if either item of luggage were to be lost.

'Have I got a pullover in there?' he asked as he pulled his jacket on. She said yes, that she had packed the beige one. As a last item, Priscilla tucked six handkerchiefs into the inside pocket of the suitcase. 'Are you taking the camera?' she asked as he put his toiletries bag into the hand luggage. He shook his head, 'Won't be time. Not much worth photographing in Bonn, anyway.' He would be away for a week and there would be a fair amount of entertaining involved so he required more clothes than were needed for his flying visits to Paris or Brussels.

The doorbell rang. They both knew that it was the taxi and their movements speeded up without losing any of their practised precision. Krista answered the door and by the time she had reached the bottom of the stairs to call them, Julian was half way down, a piece of luggage in each hand. Priscilla followed him and he turned to her quickly before going out.

'I'll try to ring Wednesday night,' he said, then hurried out the door, his raincoat over one arm. Priscilla watched the taxi driver load his suitcase into the boot while Julian climbed into the back seat. Then the taxi pulled away and she looked at her watch. Eleven-twenty. He would be at Heathrow in good time to check in for his flight.

★ ★ ★

Bertie was on the telephone as she came into the office. He grinned at her happily and carried on talking in the pitch of high excitement which had characterized most of his conversation for the past week. When the details had been settled on the Macmasters arrangement, an atmosphere of euphoric relief had overtaken all of the gallery staff. As Simon had commented, not only had their bacon been saved but the prestige which the collection would acquire was certain to enhance everybody's reputation. Bertie rang off and winked at Priscilla. 'That was David Somers. Wanted some crucial bits of information about Malvern so Macmasters would know what to say to him Sunday night.' Somers was Macmasters' personal assistant. His telephone call had been prompted by the dinner which Alistair Thurston had arranged at his London house to put the final celebratory seal on the Macmasters collection agreement which his own intervention had delivered from collapse. A building just off Grosvenor Square had hurriedly been found, the ground and first floors of which could house the collection for at least three years. Macmasters would set up a trust to pay for the short leasehold on the premises but the government, as owners, would insure and maintain the collection. An admission charge in the form of a request for donations to the trust would help toward the maintenance. Planning permission was being sought and was expected to be forthcoming. Thurston, Malvern and his Permanent Secretary had spent time closeted first with Bertie and Priscilla, then with Macmasters' solicitors, bringing the whole delicately balanced arrangement to fruition. Government backing had come partly from Environment and partly from the Arts Ministry. Thurston had, on one occasion, taken Priscilla to lunch in the Commons dining room with his Secretary of State as part of his campaign to get the cooperation of his Ministry. The solicitors were still sorting out the paper work but agreement on all major points had been reached.

Bertie sat down on the sofa and giggled. 'Macmasters is thrilled to bits with it all. He thinks this should put him well on his way to a knighthood. He wants to know all about Malvern so he can chat him up. Alistair really had him taped. Terribly sweet of him to give this dinner,' Bertie went on. 'I think we must give him something, don't you? One of those French drawings he admired the last time he came in.'

Simon had wandered into the office. He leaned on the desk where Priscilla was sitting and snickered. 'I think there's something he'd rather have.' Priscilla pulled a face and said, 'We'll give him a picture.' Simon cooed, 'Oh, he will be disappointed.' She looked at him and said, 'Would you like to oblige, dear?' Simon threw his eyes upward in mock despair. 'I'm not his type,' he sighed and walked out into the gallery to relieve the girl at the front reception desk.

The office phone rang and Bertie answered it. It was *The Times* Arts Diary wanting information about the Macmasters gift to the nation and so Bertie handed them on to Priscilla, 'who deals with our publicity.'

* * *

Priscilla drove to Cadogan Square by herself for the dinner on Sunday evening. Thurston's London home was the first two floors of one of the five-storey brick houses which lined that square. Walking up the front steps and pressing the bell, her mild nervousness was overtaken by curiosity to see what the inside of one of these houses just off Sloane Street would be like. The door was opened by a middle-aged man in a dark suit whose professional solicitude immediately identified him as a servant. He took her coat and as he turned from her, Alistair appeared from a wide doorway further down the corridor. Walking toward her, one hand outstretched to take her arm, his face conveyed the delighted, open warmth with which she had grown familiar. His manner to her over these last weeks of meetings and negotiations had become one of affectionate and relaxed friendliness. Only very occasionally had she caught a glance from him which embarrassed her with its intentness. As they proceeded down the corridor with its deep grey carpeting and mauve walls, he seized her elbow to stop her for a moment and said, 'Look, that's the picture I was telling you about.'

Above a small, highly polished rosewood table on which stood a vase of scentless hothouse flowers, there hung a painting which he had described to her at their last meeting. It was an eighteenth-century English watercolour which had, he felt, an atmosphere almost as evocative as a Turner. She agreed that it was lovely and they turned together, still commenting on the picture, into the drawing room where Macmasters and his wife, Bevis Malvern and his friend Cedric, and Charles Austin, one of Macmasters' senior partners, stood with their drinks. Malvern's voice could be heard cheerfully braying out the final lines of an anecdote which the assembled company received with appropriate peals of amusement. The servant who had taken her coat materialized at Priscilla's side and asked what she would like to drink. She requested a dry sherry and it was delivered to her on a small silver tray. The room in which they stood had walls which appeared to be a shade of rose but on close inspection, were revealed to be covered in a wallpaper of very narrow stripes of white and deep pink which fused together at any distance. At one end of it was a magnificent marble fireplace in which no fire seemed to have burnt in recent years, whose mantelpiece held what Priscilla recognized as a French ormolu clock. Some feet from the fireplace and at right angles to it, two large sofas covered in ivory silk stood facing one another. Between them was a coffee table of dark mahogany on which a silver cigarette box and several ashtrays were placed. Deeply ruched curtains in shades of ivory and pink rose and fell in luxuriant folds over and around the windows on the long wall which faced them. The crests of the curtains met the frieze of the ornate plaster ceiling, whose reliefs were pointed up by the shadowed light of the lamps sitting on their squat onyx bases. The end of the room at which they stood was furnished by several mahogany occasional tables each with its lamp and vase of flowers, and a number of spoonback chairs one of which was covered in intricate needlepoint embroidery. It intrigued Priscilla to see Thurston in this setting. His manner to her had become so disarmingly unpretentious that she found it difficult to take in the notion that after their meetings, he had returned home to this. Together they approached the small gathering of people, Thurston staying by her side. Malvern greeted her with extravagant warmth and introduced her to Cedric who smiled winsomely and offered his hand. Drawing her into the conversation, Malvern carried on with an account he had been giving to the attentive Macmasters party of an auction he had attended in Paris five years ago. Then the doorbell rang. Thurston murmured to her, 'That should be Bertie,' and gave her arm a light squeeze as he slipped out into the corridor. He returned after a moment with Bertie who carried two large parcels wrapped in brown paper.

'Bertie!' Malvern cried in enthusiastic salutation and then said with teasing incredulity. 'What *have* you got there?'

Bertie smiled coyly and said, 'I come bearing gifts.' With

fussy care, he examined the first parcel and said 'This one is for you', presenting it ceremoniously to Thurston, and then following by offering the second one to Malvern. There was a chorus of expectant appreciation and Malvern asked, 'Can we open them now, Bertie?'

'Of *course*, you may,' Bertie replied.

Malvern removed the paper and then the corrugated cardboard to reveal a pen drawing by Charles Ricketts, done as an illustration for a book by Oscar Wilde. 'Oh Bertie, how terribly sweet,' Malvern exclaimed. Cedric leaned over his shoulder and enunciated, 'Gosh, isn't it splendid.' The drawing was carefully handed round for admiration and then Malvern said, 'Open yours now, Alistair.'

Alistair removed the paper and board from his gift, handing the wrappings to Priscilla as he proceeded, in order to draw her into partnership with him. His servant hovered by her side to take them from her. With a small gasp of appreciation, Thurston looked at the exquisite Maillol pastel of a nude and then, speechless with gratitude, turned it outward for everyone to see. There were cries of acclamation and Alistair turned, genuinely touched, to thank Bertie. Immensely pleased by the success of his presents, Bertie took the whole party on to a higher gear of genial intimacy. Another round of drinks was being distributed and the first anxious stage of tentative social overture was passed.

Macmasters' attention was concentrated on Malvern, the most senior political figure present. Always having been a large contributor to Conservative funds, he was on a firm enough footing with the party hierarchy to be able to drop names which put him acceptably within Malvern's circle. They gossiped cheerfully, Malvern indulging with graceful kindness Macmasters' assiduous desire to please. Charles Austin hovered next to them, acting as a foil for his elder partner who had brought him tonight ostensibly because of his active helpfulness in the negotiations, but as well for his trustworthy support whenever Macmasters was eager to impress.

'What was that chap called, Charles, up in Edinburgh?' he was asking and Charles obliged readily, 'Sampson – Lionel

Sampson.' 'Of course,' Macmasters rejoined happily. 'Sampson – absolutely amazing little man, he was.'

Bertie and Mrs Macmasters stood with Thurston and Priscilla, their mood, thanks to Bertie's infectious good humour, taking on the relaxed familiarity of long-standing friends. Thurston's man appeared at the door to say that dinner was ready and Alistair took Priscilla's arm to lead her into the dining room, the others following in an informal procession across the corridor. The rectangular dining table, of the same highly polished mahogany as the occasional tables in the drawing room, was set in the centre of this smaller room which had walls of Wedgwood blue and a marble fireplace which matched the one in the drawing room. Alistair walked to the head of the dining table, instructing Priscilla and Mrs Macmasters to sit on either side of him. Malvern asked playfully, 'Shall I hold up the other end, Alistair?' Alistair agreed that he should. Bertie and Macmasters sat on either side of Malvern, putting Cedric between Bertie and Priscilla, Charles Austin between Mr and Mrs Macmasters.

They began with a seafood salad and a dry white wine which Priscilla could not identify although it tasted like a white Bordeaux. She was always interested in memorizing the wine selection at a dinner, for Julian's benefit since he was an avid wine buff. Cedric turned to her, put an affectionate finger on the bracelet she wore and said sweetly, 'Very pretty.'

Alistair leaned toward her. 'Let's have a look.'

She offered her wrist for his inspection and he took hold of her hand, letting his fingers close over hers for only a fraction of a second longer than was necessary. 'It is very pretty,' he said, his voice so soft that the words became ambiguous. She smiled but he could tell that she was growing wary. He had been so careful over these weeks to assume nothing so as not to offend her. If he frightened her away now by any precipitative move, he would lose his last opportunity. After tonight, there would be no legitimate means for prolonging an association with her. His restlessness before her arrival had suddenly recalled to his mind Kate's cruelly vivid description of his states of predatory excitement, and his confidence had almost disintegrated like a schoolboy before his first party. But at Priscilla's actual appearance, he was so taken by infatuation that his self-consciousness had evaporated and he was drawn into his more usual obsessive concern to make her like him. He knew that it was essential that she be fond of him. While a man might sleep with a woman simply because he found her attractive, no woman worth having would sleep with a man unless she liked him.

They moved on to pork tenderloin, and the conversation surged in waves round the table, sometimes breaking the party into small units of two or three in private exchanges, at other times sweeping the whole gathering into an audience for one triumphantly delivered monologue. At moments, a topic or a person known to them all would be under discussion at one end of the table and the other end, picking up a fragment, would relay it and the subject would be passed round like a parcel. At the peak of their high spirits, Alistair permitted himself to look at Priscilla properly while she turned to speak to Cedric. She was happily relaxed and he was so taken by her that he did not look away even when she turned back. The look she caught from him mesmerized her for a moment and he smiled at her with a private tenderness which made it impossible for her to withdraw. The fact that she did not return his smile was of no importance. They had had a moment of communication which seemed to him to be as clear as if the words had been spoken. The excitement which had been murmuring quite controllably inside him all evening, moved suddenly like an awakening creature, deep in his lower intestine. He looked down into his wine glass, prolonging the sensation, even the uncertainty of his anticipation adding somehow to its pleasure. It was the risk of disappointment, in fact, which enhanced the thrillingness of it much in the spirit that some men risked death in a dangerous sport. He would allow himself to be aroused to the limits of his self-control, knowing that the sincerity of that state would be more likely than anything else to cause her to give in to him.

Somehow, he got through the conversation over the pudding – a Pavlova, which was greeted with much praise. Then they retired to the drawing room for their coffee and liqueurs. Priscilla sat next to Bevis on one of the sofas while Thurston stood, pouring out the coffee himself. Standing in front of the fireplace, sipping his coffee, Thurston talked with Macmasters who had been accepted into the company sufficiently to be less concerned with ingratiating himself than with enjoying the evening. Priscilla listened to Bevis' charming flow of words, relieved to be removed from Thurston's disconcerting proximity. She planned to make her exit as soon as anyone else in the party departed, determined that she should not be left alone with Alistair. Liqueurs were served and she accepted a small brandy. As he handed it to her, Alistair sat down beside her in the place which had now been vacated by Malvern. He remained a respectable distance from her on the sofa but extended his arm along the back of it so that his hand was only inches from her shoulder. They talked across the coffee table to Mrs Macmasters and Bertie, who had hugely enjoyed himself, even succeeded in re-establishing his dealings with Malvern, who promised to visit the gallery the following week to see some paintings which Bertie thought might interest him. Priscilla glanced at Alistair covertly. Leaning back in his sofa, he looked completely at home in this beautiful room and she felt a surge of exaltation in the knowledge that he was in pursuit of her. Even the transitory, superficial hold over him that a physical attraction provided seemed, in her lapse into girlish adulation, to be worth savouring. It was the ultimate seductive power of his position of which Thurston was barely aware: that a man who could have anything should want her, out of all that it was possible to want. He turned then and caught the last seconds of her glance.

Bertie was the first to make a move, extending his affectionate goodbye to everyone in the room. Macmasters and his wife began to make restive preparatory noises as well and Priscilla mentally readied herself, although she made no actual move as yet. It would have been rude to have broken up the party definitively so she allowed herself a further quarter of an hour. Then, at the time she had appointed for herself, Malvern rose and said, 'Must be off, Alistair ... lovely evening.' He said 'good night' to Priscilla and she said, 'I'll go out with you,' as he and Cedric walked toward the drawing room door. But Alistair caught her arm. 'Don't go. I wanted to show you the pictures in the library that you've heard so much about.'

She was caught off guard and in her hesitation, Malvern

rushed in, 'Oh, *do* have a look. He's got some wonderful things . . . a super Freud portrait.' It was impossible now to refuse and so she stood back as Cedric and Bevis were seen out by Alistair. She had only a moment alone before Alistair returned through the door. He smiled at her with infinite kindness, seeming more relaxed in direct proportion to her increased anxiety. Extending his arm to lead her there, he said, 'The library's at the end of the corridor.' She went to him and he put his arm around her waist for the first time that evening. They walked the length of the corridor to a set of double doors at its end. He reached out and opened one of them, then let her pass through in front of him. She entered into the dark and as he came in behind her, he reached for the light switch and the room suddenly spread before her, end walls lined to the ceiling with books, the long walls hung, between their large windows, with pictures. He walked to one end of the room, across the polished floorboards with their scattering of Oriental rugs and motioned for her to follow. When she approached, he pointed out the Freud portrait, a Hodgkin, and his favourite early French landscape. She took them in with apparent concentration but he sensed that she was genuinely frightened, and felt strengthened by his own protectiveness. 'What's the matter?' he asked, his voice soft with concern. She cast her eyes down and, as so often before, he found her diffidence more arousing than any open invitation. He touched her back tenderly and said, 'I won't hurt you,' in a voice which conveyed real humaneness. She said nothing but he could feel her trembling against his hand. He took hold of her arms very gently and turned her round to face him. 'You're not afraid of me are you?' He sounded both comforting and hurt. He was enough of a gentleman, and sufficiently vain, not to want to terrorize her into submission. She shook her head but said nothing, still standing completely still where he had put her, as if she were too petrified to move. He looked at her for a moment. Her eyes avoided his face but he still held her arms and she made no move to push him away. He bent down and kissed her neck, then moved upwards along her face until he met her mouth. But with the contact of their lips, she pulled away from him as if she had abruptly snapped into consciousness. Startled by her sudden movement, he recovered in time to catch her in his arms before she could flee out of his reach. He was desperately in need of her now, feeling with complete conviction that he would not be able to survive her rejection. He pulled her against him firmly and kissed her, forcing her mouth to open for him. She pulled her head back but he still held her pressed against him. 'Please,' he whispered wretchedly. She could feel the hardness of his groin pressing into her pelvis and knew how cruel it would be to turn him away. Nearly in tears, she begged him to stop but he still held her, frantically repeating his reassurance, at first imploringly then more firmly as he felt her subside. Finding her mouth once again, he penetrated it this time without resistance. Then slowly, he drew back and took her hand to lead her from the room. The guest bedroom was next door to the library. A bedside lamp was lit when they entered and she wondered later whether that room had been prepared in readiness for her. Once inside the door, aware that it would take more strength than she possessed to back out now, she stood unmoving unable to go either forward or backward in this act to which she had acquiesced. Alistair took off his jacket, then walked up behind her and reached with practised expertise for the zip on the back of her dress. She shut her eyes like a child as he unzipped it. Slipping his hands inside the dress, he brought them round to the front of her waist and then up to her breasts as he bent forward to kiss her back. She was shaking violently, incapable of removing her own clothes, so he slid the dress down over her shoulders and on to the floor, then unhooked her bra so that he could feel her bare breasts with his hands. Finally, she stepped out of her dress and removed the rest of her clothes while he watched her. When she was completely naked, he came up to her still dressed and smoothed his hands from her breasts down over her body. She gasped as he reached her groin and that response brought him to the point where he could delay no longer. He turned down the covers of the bed for her and she lay down while he undressed. He made love to her with all the finesse and control of which he was capable and when the final violence of intercourse overtook him, he was delighted to find that he had satisfied her.

As soon as it was over, she turned her face away from him

while he still lay on top of her, closing her eyes so that she would not have to look at him. He touched her face with his hand and then kissed her eyelids but she would not turn to him. 'Open your eyes,' he said with quiet firmness and she obeyed him. Turning her head to make her meet his gaze, he said, 'Don't worry. Nothing's going to happen. It's our secret and it's perfectly safe.' His voice had the unwavering clarity with which one would reassure a child or an hysteric. He was so confident that she found she could believe him, and he felt her relax under him.

Now that his frantic desire had been eased, he could enjoy her body with more comfortable indulgence. He moved off her and ran his hand slowly down from her breasts to her thighs, pleased that it aroused her again. He leaned over her to kiss her waist and she shuddered. 'Do you want me to make love to you again?' he whispered, and was so overjoyed when she nodded her head that he was immediately capable of penetrating her once more. This time he was slower and more deliberate, enhancing all of her pleasures and prolonging her climax until she was satiated. He dropped down next to her then, exhausted and utterly elated. The knowledge that he had had to engage in as much coercion as had been necessary the first time was erased by the fact that the second time had been by invitation. She was lying quietly next to him, with her arm across her face. He reached over to her, laying his hand on her stomach. 'Can you stay for the night?' he asked hopefully.

The assumption in his question made her appallingly aware of how different their lives and expectations were. It broke the unreal haze into which he had transported her. She shook her head. 'What time is it?' she asked. He looked at the clock on the bedside table. 'Ten to three,' he said. She pushed against her fatigue and sat up. He caught her wrist as she was about to leave the bed. 'Is your husband there?' he asked bluntly. She shook her head. 'He's away.'

'Who's at home now with your children?'

'The au pair.'

'Will she be waiting up for you?'

Priscilla shook her head.

'Then there's no hurry. Don't go yet.' He said it with such

matter-of-fact authority and she was so tired, that she gave in to him without further objection and lay back down on the bed. Her submissiveness was driving him wild with adoration. If he had been attracted before, the control that he was discovering he could have over her, was undoing him completely. He longed for her to be as happy as he was, to have no regrets, to admit that she had wanted him. He turned on his side, put an arm around her waist and kissed her hair. 'Are you all right?' he asked her. She nodded. 'Speak to me, then,' he said, moving his hand down on to her stomach. She still would not turn to him, 'What do you want me to say?' He thought for a moment of what he actually wanted her to say. She could read his thoughts as clearly as if he had spoken them but she would not give him the satisfaction of saying what he wanted to hear. He slid his hand down to her groin and she stiffened, reaching down to stop him. He smiled but would not stop. 'Tell me that you want me,' he whispered. She writhed against his hand and said hurriedly, 'Yes, I do.' Then he stopped and kissed her with passionate tenderness.

It was half-past four by the time she got home, letting herself into the house as noiselessly as possible. She fell into her own bed, so exhausted that she could have no clear thoughts about what had happened to her. As she fell asleep, her last reflections were of frantic gratitude that she would have a week in which to put this out of her mind before Julian returned.

After he had seen her out through the darkened house, Alistair had returned to his own bedroom upstairs, too tired even to shower. He stretched out luxuriantly in the fresh bed, the coolness of the sheets easing his aching fatigue. There was a peculiar euphoric calm about moments like these. He felt more at peace with himself than was possible at any other time, the hunted, churning anxiety which always seemed to lie in wait for him put temporarily to rest. He knew that he had entered into a really consuming passion and he lay awake, his mind in a pleasantly incoherent state of semi-consciousness, anticipating future meetings and wondering whether it would ever be feasible for her to get away for weekends. His few serious affairs had always been with married women. Although the practical arrangements were more difficult there was additional safety in the fact that the woman's interests were also in secrecy, she having as much concern as he to avoid exposure. As well, although this was largely unconscious, he found married women more attractive. They were invariably more sympathetic and perceptive than single women, understood the contingencies of men's lives and did not make silly, girlish demands. Already having husbands of their own, they had no desire to play wife to another man, but could enjoy a love affair for the circumscribed thing that it was. He fell asleep longing to see Priscilla and resolving to ring her at the gallery the next morning to make sure she had got home safely.

★ ★ ★

It was half-past ten on Monday morning when he first rang, to be told that Priscilla had not yet arrived at the gallery but that she was expected later. He left a message saying that he had telephoned and that he would ring back. He had a series of appointments through the morning which took him to half-past twelve. Just before leaving for a working lunch, he tried the gallery again. She had come in but gone out again. They did not know when she would be back.

There was a select committee meeting in the afternoon at which he had to appear. After lunch, he was closeted with Harvey Wynne and three other Ministry officials, being briefed for his appearance. At three, the car arrived to take him to the House for his committee meeting. They gave him a rough ride and he did not emerge from the committee room until after four. It was four-thirty before he was back in his office. He telephoned the gallery once more to be told that Priscilla had gone off for an appointment and was intending to go straight home from there, and yes, she had been given the message that he had telephoned.

When he rang off, he looked so downcast that Harvey Wynne, sitting across the room, asked him if there was anything wrong. Alistair shook his head and said, his voice lightly wistful, 'I'm madly in love, that's all.'

'Oh, dear,' Harvey murmured wryly. Alistair pulled himself out of his fit of melancholy and opened his junior minister's black box to retrieve the committee papers. He knew Priscilla's home telephone number but it was inconceivable to use it. There was nothing he could do now except wait until tomorrow.

★ ★ ★

Priscilla arrived at the gallery at eleven on Tuesday morning to the message that Alistair Thurston had rung, and could she ring him on his private ministry number when she got in. 'Do ring him,' Simon said. 'He's getting very persistent.' But she did not ring him, repeating her instruction to all of the gallery staff that she was not in, to anyone who telephoned. She went out to lunch at their usual pub with Simon and the receptionist. When they got back at half-past two there were two dozen roses waiting for her at the reception desk. 'Oh, gosh,' Simon said, 'aren't you the favoured one.' The card with them was simply signed, 'A.T.' Priscilla took the flowers into the office and Simon filled a vase with water for her. When she had arranged them, she put the vase on top of the filing cabinet instead of on her own desk.

'But they're meant for you,' Simon protested. 'Never mind,' she said and prepared to leave to go to the photographer's to see some contact prints the gallery had had done.

'What shall we say if he rings again?' Simon chirped mischievously as she went out the door. 'Say that I'm not here,' she replied. She successfully eluded him for the remainder of that day and for the first half of Wednesday. But at lunchtime, the receptionist went out early to meet her boyfriend, Bertie was away for the day and Simon was out as well, so that at half-past twelve she found herself alone in the gallery when the telephone rang. As soon as she answered it, she knew that it was him. There was the briefest silence on the other end of the telephone as he recognized her voice, then he said, 'Priscilla?'

'Yes.' She remained standing even though there was a chair next to her.

'How are you?' His voice was soft and apprehensive.

'I'm all right,' she replied, adding nothing more.

'I want to see you,' he said, sounding terse with panic at her coldness.

'I can't.'

He was stunned into silence for a moment and his voice was hoarse when it returned. 'Priscilla, please. I want to talk to you.'

'I'm sorry,' she said, her tone cool and final. 'I can't. Please don't try to see me.' Then she put the telephone down. Her calm disintegrated as soon as she had rung off. She sat down, shaking but intensely relieved that it was over. The sound of his voice had brought back with horrific clarity all the details which she had been attempting to forget. In her own self-concern she had hardly taken in his words but his manner had surprised her. He seemed genuinely upset where she would have expected more worldly cynicism. She was still sitting in the same place when Simon got back forty minutes later.

'What's wrong?' he asked as soon as he saw her. She shook her head and said, 'Nothing,' more decisively than she felt. He continued to look at her, obviously alarmed by the expression on her face. Before he could persevere with his questions, the sound of a familiar girlish laugh could be heard out in the gallery. Debbie Ackerman appeared at the office door. She was tanned, expensively dressed and obviously extremely happy.

'Hi,' she said to Priscilla with such effusiveness that, even in her present state of mind, Priscilla was warmed by it.

'How are you?' Priscilla asked unnecessarily since Debbie was clearly ecstatically well.

'I'm just great,' she answered. 'Hey look, have you had lunch yet?' It occurred to Priscilla then that she had not. She shook her head.

'Well, come on then,' Debbie said with a determination that could not be questioned. 'I'm going to take you out to lunch.'

'Are you?' Priscilla asked, slightly nonplussed but so in need of succour that Debbie's affection was irresistible.

'Go on,' Simon said kindly. 'It'll do you good.' Priscilla stood up without further comment to get her jacket.

It was beginning to feel like spring outside. The persistent April rain was giving way to sudden warm bursts of sunshine. As they walked to the wine bar, the pavements were drying from the last shower. Debbie looked like the season in her pink jumper and skirt.

'Where have you been?' Priscilla asked, referring to her

unseasonal tan. Debbie grinned. 'The Bahamas.' Then she said, 'I'll tell you all about it.' They went down the steep flight of stairs to the crowded basement where tables covered in red tablecloths held noisily gregarious parties meeting for professional lunches. A black uniformed waitress approached them. Having nearly to shout over the noise which rebounded off the bare brick walls and low ceiling, she asked how many they were and then led them to a small table in an alcove where the din was more muted. They ordered sirloin steaks on Debbie's insistence and a bottle of claret.

Debbie chewed on a breadstick and beamed across the table. 'Do you want to hear my news?' Priscilla looked up obligingly.

'I've been with Harry full-time since I met him with you that night.'

'Have you?' Priscilla was shocked not only by the information but by the uncomplicated happiness which the situation seemed to entail for Debbie.

'I've been staying at his flat on and off.' She giggled. 'He wants me there all the time but I go back to my own place a couple of times a week.' Then she added, 'And when he goes home for weekends.'

Priscilla was completely at a loss for words. The question she wanted to ask, *do you really like him*, was unsayable. As if she had read Priscilla's thoughts, Debbie said, 'He's the nicest man I've ever been with. We had an amazing trip.'

'It was Harry who took you to the Bahamas?'

Debbie nodded. 'He's really great to me,' she said with a tenderness that was patently sincere, 'And,' she added significantly, 'the *Daily News* is publishing my Harold Lewis interview.'

Their steaks and salads arrived and Priscilla began to eat with more energy than she would have thought possible an hour before. There was something about Debbie's animation and gaiety which was infectious even though the source of it seemed to her so disturbing. She found herself wondering, as the food and wine restored some centre of gravity to the hollow unease which had taken her over, whether or not she was appalled at what Debbie was telling her and, if she was, why that should be so. In some amorphous, unspecific way she felt herself turning over and examining some of her most basic assumptions.

'He's sending me out to do a lot of arts features now.' Debbie was going on. 'They haven't got an arts editor on the *Daily News*, so if I play my cards right, I could end up with a really good job.' Priscilla thought of Harry Fitzjohn, a thoroughly presentable – even attractive in a rather bumptious way – and certainly impressively influential man in late middle age. What a delight it must be for him to be given the adoration, as total as Debbie would know how to give it, of a beautiful and lively young woman. *He must be besotted*, Priscilla thought with some pity. She looked at Debbie as closely as she thought permissible, trying to discern her true feelings. She seemed as innocently blissful as a bride. Was she, at least in some sense, in love? Or did that not even come into it for her in this kind of situation. Priscilla felt herself to be, for the first time in years, something of an ingenue.

'I did a piece on the Docklands Arts Complex but it was unsigned,' Debbie was saying now. 'Just a description to go with the photospread. He was very pleased with it.'

Priscilla finished her meal and helped herself to the last of the wine. The agony of the last few days was beginning to retreat into tolerable indistinctness and Debbie's revelations were putting her experience into a different perspective. She began to feel childish for having become so distraught about what was now beginning to seem like a trivial incident. She wondered what Debbie would make of it if she were to confide her own little adventure to her. *Good for you – how was it?* she would say. For a moment, she almost considered telling her, longing to normalize the situation by bringing it into Debbie's reassuring frame of reference. But she thought better of it and they parted on the corner of Bond Street with promises to meet again soon.

Julian rang home late that night as he had promised he would try to do. Fresh from her triumphant refusal of Thurston, she could talk to him easily. He told her about the meetings he had had on Monday and Tuesday, the hotel he was staying in, the client he had visited at the weekend, sounding immensely pleased with the progress he was making. He said that he was flying back on Saturday and she took the details of the flight so that she could collect him at Heathrow. She wished him luck with the new client he was seeing on Friday and they said a cheerful goodbye. For the first time since the previous Saturday, she went to bed and slept soundly.

★ ★ ★

She went in to the gallery at ten on Thursday, spending the morning at her desk. Every time that the telephone rang, she shut her eyes, praying that it would not be Thurston. By lunch time, she was beginning to feel that perhaps she had succeeded in putting him off. His pride would be such, she told herself, that an outright rejection would be beyond endurance. She went down to the basement at half-past twelve to bring up some prints for a client whom Bertie was meeting for lunch. It took a quarter of an hour to locate the three lithographs he had requested. She carried them upstairs and as she walked back toward the office, she could hear Bertie talking animatedly. Assuming that his client had arrived, she quickened her pace.

Fortunately, Alistair had his back to her as she reached the office door so that he did not see her freeze at the sight of him. She had only a few seconds to compose her face because Bertie, looking over Thurston's shoulder, announced cheerfully, 'Here she is!' Alistair turned. There were such signs of strain in his facial expression that she felt a throb of something like sympathy which made her less afraid, and she was able to walk past him into the office with an appearance of composure. Handing the prints to Bertie, she went to her desk and leaned against the edge of it for support but did not sit down, knowing that Alistair would have to remain standing as long as she did. Bertie continued to chat amiably and then Simon came in as well and greeted Thurston. 'What can we do for you?' Simon asked pleasantly.

'Nothing,' Alistair replied with a smile which approached his usual smoothness. 'I've just come to take Priscilla to lunch.'

'Oh, how nice,' Simon said, avoiding Priscilla's eyes. Alistair turned to face her then for the first time. She looked too shocked even to be annoyed and, seizing the moment, he took hold of her arm and said in a voice whose warmth was unrefusable, 'I've booked a table around the corner.' When she did not protest, he added gently, 'Go and get your coat.' She did as he said, dumbfounded but flattered, in spite of herself, by his determination.

He ushered her out the door and neither of them spoke as they made their way to a French restaurant half a block away, whose most charming feature was a conservatory which, even in spring, trapped the sun sufficiently to be warm. He had taken a small table in the corner of this glass domed room. The plants which hung from its ceiling and lined the edges of the tiled floor, made the lukewarm sunshine feel almost tropical in its beneficence. With its cane furniture and pretty ambience, the restaurant had an engaging cheerfulness, seeming to transport a bit of summer into the day. The waiter guided them to their chairs and asked if they would like a drink.

'Perrier?' Alistair asked her, knowing that it was what she always requested at lunch. She nodded. He asked for a whisky for himself and drank it quickly when it came, then turned to her as the waiter left. She returned his look but said nothing, keeping her face resolutely expressionless.

'Don't be angry with me,' he said quietly.

She sighed in exasperation at his inexhaustible ability to gain the advantage. 'Alistair,' she said, as if she were growing impatient with a child of whom she was basically fond, 'you shouldn't have done this.'

'I had to,' he said simply. 'You wouldn't speak to me.' She shut her eyes, speechless, but more relaxed. He seemed so unnerved that it increased her confidence and in her strength, she felt benevolent towards him. Another waiter arrived then to take their order. She looked at the menu for the first time and made an instant decision which she immediately forgot so that when the food came she could not recall having ordered it. After the waiter had gone, Alistair turned back to her. He looked, she realized, really drawn. 'Are you all right?' she asked. 'You don't look very well.' He was slightly embarrassed but then, giving her a pointed look, said, 'That's because I haven't slept for two nights.' He was pleased to see that she seemed pained by this admission. He gave her a longer, more frankly appreciative gaze and said, 'You look extremely well.'

She wanted to say that what had happened had cost her a few nights' sleep as well, that what suffering she was causing him he had brought on himself but he looked too fragile to invite any cruelty, and she could not make a scene in the middle of a restaurant. His soup and the melon she had apparently ordered, arrived at the table. While the waiter fussed around them with bread rolls and cutlery, nothing could be said. The Beaujolais which Alistair had requested was delivered, offered to him to taste, then poured into their glasses. Finally, they were left to themselves again.

'Is your husband back yet?' he asked. She was reluctant to answer him but said at last, 'No, he gets back on Saturday.' He drank some of his wine. The effects of the alcohol on a nearly empty stomach were helping him to overcome his nervous paralysis. It suddenly seemed to him that there was nothing that he could say, except what he felt. His voice was soft but very deliberate. 'I can't face not seeing you any more.' Priscilla laid her fork down and put a hand over her eyes. He went on very quietly, 'I adore you. I've wanted . . .' But she cut into his speech in a desperate whisper, 'Stop it Alistair, please.' He stopped but when she could bear to look at him, he was so obviously distressed, that her resolve nearly weakened. He was almost succeeding in making her feel that she had wounded him in a fit of callous whimsy.

The waiter descended to remove their first course dishes and refill their wine glasses. Alistair rubbed his hands over his eyes suddenly and she asked him, not unkindly, what was the matter. He shook his head and said, 'Nothing, just a bit dizzy. Drinking too fast.' She had to fight against an impulse to reach over and touch his face and even though she refrained, he seemed to sense her desire to do so and was comforted by it. Their main courses arrived. He began to eat, realizing that he was really hungry for the first time in days. The food made him feel better, neutralizing the alcohol and countering his fatigue. He looked across at Priscilla and waited for her to meet his eyes. Then he said, in a voice still tentative but more like his normal one, 'I've bought that Bonnard print we saw at Colnaghi's.' It was a small, early lithograph which they had seen and admired together. The significance of his having bought it was not lost on her. 'It's being framed,' he went on. 'I'm getting it next week.' She did not say anything but her silence was no longer hostile. Finally, she relented and said, 'It's a very nice print.' He resisted the temptation to invite her to his house to help him decide where it should hang, but he was warmed by the conviction that he would, soon enough, do exactly that, and that when he did she would accept.

* * *

His next approach to her would have to have some urgency. He had always known that, not with overt calculation but a vague instinctual awareness. And now, here it was, the perfect opportunity. He had been laid low by illness for four days, the Green Paper on housing which had been prepared under his management and released with great publicity was taking a battering in the press (even *The Times*, normally so helpful to this government, had called it 'half-baked and sadly misjudged') and he was genuinely desolate. It was with real longing for the sound of her voice that he rang the gallery. By some miracle, she answered the telephone herself.

'Priscilla?' he asked, his voice unnecessarily tentative since he knew instantly that it was her.

'Yes,' she said familiarly. He was pleased that she also recognized him, unaware that she had been anticipating this telephone call with dreadful excitement for days. 'I need to see you.' His tone was sombre, referring to other contingencies, not just a predictable request.

'What's wrong?' she asked.

'I'm going under.' He hesitated. Then, 'I've been ill for the past week. My department's being hauled over the coals and things are going to pieces around me.' His throat was dry from the sickness which had beleaguered him, his voice flat and defeated.

'I'm sorry,' she said and the sweetness of her words felt like a warm blanket being wrapped around him.

'Please come over,' he almost whispered. 'Just to talk.' Then he added to stress the innocence of his invitation, 'I need some company.'

'Alistair,' she began to protest but her voice was already giving way.

'Just, stay for an hour. My PPS is coming over at five,

anyway,' he persevered. It was now after three. There would scarcely be time for anything but talk.

'All right,' she said rather primly like a parent granting a limited request. 'I'll be there about four.' That would give them less than an hour together since she would clearly have to be well out of the way before his Parliamentary Private Secretary arrived.

In fact, it was a few minutes past four when she rang his doorbell. She had parked on a meter and put in only enough money for an hour, as if to manifest her own conviction. Alistair came to the door himself. He had showered and shaved for her visit, noting in the mirror his pallor and sunken eyes, aware that his face would reinforce the description he had given of his condition. He saw her take in his appearance and soften her assumed aloofness as she came through the door.

Without a word he led her to the living room, touching her arm with gentlemanly inoffensiveness. She sat down on one of the cream sofas, surprisingly at home in this room where she had been only once before. Seeing it in daylight made it seem, while still opulent, somehow more ordinary and less theatrically flawless. There was a crazing of fine cracks in the corner of the ceiling and a small faded stain on the carpet under the coffee table. The thin light of an overcast day spread the same grey, dull illumination over this room as it did over her own living room, showing up its mild imperfections. Alistair sat next to her on the sofa but at a respectful distance.

'How are you?' he asked, the softness of his voice making the question intimate.

'I'm fine,' she said. 'But you obviously aren't.' He winced in reply, not wishing to avert her sympathy by demurring.

'What is it?' she asked, meaning his illness.

He shrugged. 'The doctor says either gastro-enteritis or an incipient ulcer. If it isn't better soon, they're going to x-ray my stomach.'

'Have you had this sort of thing before?' Her voice was concerned.

He nodded. 'Occasionally. I think it's just my personal reaction to stress.' The living room door opened and Alistair's man appeared with a tea tray which he deposited as quietly as was humanly possible on the occasional table at the opposite end of the room. He then vanished so silently that had Priscilla not been facing in his direction, she would scarcely have been aware that he was in the room. But Alistair who had not been looking toward the necessary spot seemed nonetheless to have perceived the arrival of the tray.

'Would you like some tea?' he asked, his solicitousness seeming particularly gallant in the face of his debilitation. She nodded and then watched him walk the length of the room. He was wearing an open-necked shirt and pullover with a pair of corduroy trousers, an outfit quite like the kind that Julian would wear at the weekends except that Alistair's sweater was probably cashmere and the shirt handmade. As he stood with his back to her, pouring out tea she gazed, quite unconsciously, at his body, the square shoulders, long back, broadening waist and then the narrowness again of his hips, vestiges of a thin boyhood. She had a sudden vivid memory of how he had looked naked, the surprising whiteness of his skin, an older and heavier man than her husband with slender arms but the beginning of a hemispherical belly. He turned around holding their cups of tea and saw her looking at him. When he returned to the sofa he sat closer to her.

'You've had a bad time from the press,' she ventured sympathetically over the tea. His face fell into frank despair. 'It's a mess,' he murmured. She waited for him to go on, flattered by the openness of his manner, his willingness to confide even what might be politically indiscreet. 'We were caught in a pincer movement. Number Ten wanted really radical proposals for private housing associations to take over public responsibilities. The Department officials dragged their feet and made it unworkable. We compromised and ended up with a dog's dinner.'

She listened gravely and then said, 'How serious is it for you?'

He shrugged eloquently. 'I'll have to get through the worst the Opposition can throw at me in Question Time and do a lot of fancy footwork with the media. If I ride it successfully, it could be all right.'

'And if not?' she asked wryly.

'If not, not.'

'It's because you're not well that things look so bleak,' she said gently. 'I'm sure you're up to the footwork. You always come over very well on television interviews.'

'Do I?' he asked with pleased surprise.

'Of course you do.' She gave him an admonishing look, thinking it was false modesty. 'Very smooth and competent.'

He grinned with pleasure and embarrassment. 'I thought I just seemed glib.' She laughed lightly. 'It amounts to the same thing in politicians, doesn't it?'

'Now, now,' he scolded her but he was delighted by her relaxed good humour. To be more substantially helpful, she said, 'Aren't civil servants notorious for obstructing radical proposals? It's not really all your fault, is it?' He nodded over his tea cup. 'We've had some sympathy. The Chief Whip said to me "Don't worry, old boy. They're a hard bunch of buggers at the DoE. The PM doesn't expect miracles. We'll clear the air a bit and have another shove".'

She beamed encouragement. It was like listening to Julian's accounts of office politics. 'All you have to do is keep your head, don't you?' She said this with cautious optimism knowing that he was in real danger.

'Yes,' he agreed wistfully. 'All I have to do is keep my head.' Then he added ruefully, 'And get my tummy sorted out.' He put his empty teacup down on the coffee table and leaned back against the sofa looking drained and grey.

'Are you feeling ill?' she asked, so tenderly that he seemed to feel her breathe as she spoke. It was as if she had touched him with her voice. He shook his head but kept his eyes shut, holding his breath to sustain this moment of ecstasy in her complete unambivalent attention, imagining for a moment that she might kiss him. But she said and did nothing more, although her presence was a palpable warmth ready to enfold him. Opening his eyes, he turned to her, started to speak and then realized that he had no words prepared. She was alarmed now, worried that she had allowed him to perceive too much. 'I've got to leave.' It was said with apology but unanswerable firmness.

'All right,' he said quietly. To argue would be fatal. She

would come again. He stood up to see her out. They walked down the long hall without speaking. At the door she turned to him and said with an affectionate smile, 'I hope you're better.'

He touched her face and ran a finger down to her mouth. There was a vibration in the muscle of her cheek. 'I won't kiss you,' he said, 'in case I'm infectious.' She stood still, looking at him until he smiled and said very quietly, 'Unless you want me to.' She said nothing, only gazed at him as if she were trying to read something in his eyes. He waited for a further second, giving her time. His movements were very slow as he put his arms around her, without haste or coercion. She was shaking and he was steadying her. He pulled her against him. 'It's all right,' he whispered against the top of her head. Then he leant down and kissed her softly with closed lips at first, then when she showed no resistance, penetrating her mouth. When he drew away, she looked so white that he was afraid she might faint. 'What's the matter?' he whispered. She shook her head to say that nothing was wrong but she was shivering and he enclosed her in his arms as if to warm and protect her. 'I won't let anything happen to you. Don't be frightened.' Her face was against his chest and she felt his voice as if it were inside her head. Putting his hands on either side of her face, he looked down at her and said, 'You'd better leave now. Harvey's on his way.' It was a promise, not only of further meetings but of his conscientiousness in guarding their secret. She pulled away, still silent. Wanting her to speak, he said, 'I'll ring you at the gallery tomorrow.' She nodded and he lifted one of her hands to his mouth and kissed the palm to seal their understanding.

Part Three

'I WOULDN'T MIND IT so much if he had some idea of what he wanted to *do*,' Rachel said, accepting the mug of coffee which Priscilla offered to her. 'He hangs around the house all day and then goes out at night until all hours. Sometimes he doesn't come back until the next day and, of course, if I ask him to ring home to say where he is, *I'm* being authoritarian and trying to control his life.'

Rachel's son, who had dropped out of school after failing four of his six 'O' levels, dominated her thoughts at the moment. Sitting in Priscilla's quiet kitchen after the Friday morning shop at Sainsbury's, she indulged her anxiety. 'Peter says we have to be patient with him, that he needs space in which to find himself.'

Priscilla, reflecting on the Jupps' house, thought that space seemed to be Peter's answer to everything. But she said, 'Up to a point.'

'Exactly,' Rachel concurred triumphantly. 'You can have so much space that you get lost in it.'

'Yes, you can,' Priscilla said.

'I mean,' Rachel went on, 'there have to be *limits*. Everybody has to have limits to their behaviour in order to make sense of their lives.'

'The problem is,' Priscilla answered, 'knowing which limits

are the right ones.' Rachel, not knowing Priscilla's private train of thought, countered, 'But for kids – and he is still a kid, whatever he thinks – the limits have got to be set by the home. When they're independent adults they can opt out and live as they like but as long as you're responsible for them, the standards have to come from you. Don't you think so?'

Priscilla seemed to start at having a question directed at her. 'Oh, yes,' she agreed quickly, 'I do.'

Misunderstanding her distraction, Rachel smiled and said, 'All these problems must seem very remote to you. You just wait another ten years.' Priscilla smiled back at her, envious of the fact that Rachel at least had a problem which she felt free to discuss. For a wild moment she wondered how Rachel would react if she were to say, *I'm having an affair with a man who won't go away and to tell you the truth, I don't want him to.*

Rachel, in her preoccupation, noticed nothing in Priscilla's manner. 'He says one week that he wants to go into the music business and the next week that he wants to go to art school and after that he's interested in computing. And he won't pursue *anything* properly.'

'He's only sixteen,' Priscilla countered mildly.

'Nearly seventeen, actually,' Rachel corrected her. 'In the working class a generation ago, he'd have been expected to be earning a living by now. And time is slipping away. He's wasted a year. It will be harder and harder for him to make up the lost time, the longer it goes on.' She finished her coffee and placed the mug down on the pine table, fingering the rim of it absently. 'The bloody trouble is, the system is so ruthless. Once you drop out, it's so hard to get back in. It doesn't seem right that making one mistake should put you beyond the pale for all time, does it?'

Priscilla looked at her for a moment, struck by the sudden irrational thought that Rachel knew, that her words were directed at her. But the innocent unambiguousness of Rachel's expression made it apparent that the idea was ludicrous. 'Of course, it shouldn't,' Priscilla replied with conviction.

There was the sound of a key turning in the front door upstairs and then a burst of excited four-year-old chatter as Emily ran into the house above their heads. 'Mummy,' she called out when she was barely through the door.

'I'm down here,' Priscilla shouted and even before she had completed the words, Emily's curly head was bobbing down the stairs. Friday was the only weekday that Priscilla was at home for Emily's return from playgroup and they both looked forward to the few hours alone together before Jaimie got back from school. Krista had Friday afternoons off so that their privacy was complete and Emily, prizing her special time, dispensed ruthlessly with Krista's attentions immediately upon arriving in the house. As Emily climbed onto her lap, Priscilla said, 'Have you got your pictures?' Emily nodded slowly, gazing at Rachel with the pacific, almost sleepy calm of a child in her mother's arms. 'Where are they?' Priscilla asked. 'I want to see them.' Emily always brought her week's art work home on a Friday. 'Krista has them,' Emily replied.

'Those are very smart shoes,' Rachel said, pointing to Emily's feet. 'They're not shoes, they're sandals,' Emily corrected with four-year-old pedantry.

'I beg your pardon,' Rachel apologized. 'When did you get them?'

'Yesterday,' Emily said proudly.

Krista came down the stairs, a carrier bag full of shopping in one hand and Emily's folder of pictures in the other. Emily glanced at her indifferently.

'Aren't you going to get your paintings for me?' Priscilla whispered into her ear, nuzzling her face against the softness of Emily's neck. Climbing down from her lap, Emily went to fetch her pictures. While Krista put the shopping away in the fridge, Emily spread the large pieces of paper from her folder carefully on the table. There were several paintings with large streaks of colour evenly distributed over the paper, one picture composed of glued bits of coloured string and a number of collages, which were called 'stickings' at playgroup, made with all manner of things from fragments of cloth and foil to pieces of macaroni.

'How lovely,' Rachel cried enthusiastically as Emily gazed down impassively at her accomplishments. 'Perhaps one day you'll do something that will hang in Mummy's art gallery.' Emily looked at her, as unmoved by this idea as she was by the works themselves.

'That's a particularly nice one,' Priscilla said, pointing to a painting with swirling strokes of blue across it. 'Shall we hang it on the pinboard?' Emily nodded her assent and Priscilla proceeded to add it to the collection of pictures which covered the cork board on one kitchen wall. The telephone rang and Priscilla reached over to it.

'How are you?' Rachel heard her say. Then, 'Really, what's the matter?' in a concerned voice. 'Oh, dear,' she went on, turning to Rachel with a wry face. Rachel smiled at her quizzically. 'Have you called them yet?' Priscilla was asking. There was a long pause while Priscilla listened. 'They can't come until *Wednesday*?' she said with sympathetic alarm. Rachel looked at her and Priscilla glanced heavenward in mock despair. 'Well, you'll just have to cope with the laundromat, won't you?' Rachel snickered. 'Oh, God,' Priscilla continued her commiseration. Emily, growing impatient at the loss of her mother's attention, pulled at her hand fretfully. 'I doubt that it will do any damage if you mopped it up straightaway.' Emily buried her face in Priscilla's thigh and began to make loudly complaining noises. 'I'm going to have to go, Beth,' Priscilla apologized. 'Emily's just got back from playgroup.' There was a further pause in which Priscilla knelt down and put her arm around Emily to pacify her while still holding the phone to her ear. 'Well look, why don't you ring a few other places and see if you can get someone round sooner . . . The yellow pages are full of them . . . under Washing Machine Repairs . . . okay. I really must go now, Beth. Speak to you next week . . . I hope you get sorted out. 'Bye.' She stood up to replace the receiver of the telephone and then immediately scooped Emily up in her arms. Rachel was grinning when they returned to the table. 'I do wish I had as much drama in my life as Beth manages to have in hers,' she said.

Priscilla sighed. 'I wish that my biggest problem was a collapsed washing machine.' There was something in her voice that made Rachel look at her. Feeling that they were close enough friends to justify the query, she said quietly, 'Is anything the matter?' Priscilla hesitated but only for a second. 'No,' she said. Then she added lightly, 'Just the pressures of a working mother.' Rachel smiled kindly but months later she would recall that conversation with new understanding.

* * *

Alistair had stopped speaking. He leant his elbows on the table and looked across at her with the undisguised adoration which he was now licensed to reveal, his silence adding to the pointedness of his gaze. Unnerved as she always was by that expression on his face, Priscilla said, 'What's the matter?'

'Nothing,' he replied softly. 'Why should anything be the matter?'

'You were looking at me strangely.'

He shrugged. 'I was just looking at you.'

She smiled but less comfortably than he had. 'Don't you have to go?' she asked. It was Thursday and he was driving back to Yorkshire that afternoon for a long weekend. It had been impossible for them to meet earlier in the week and finally, unable to bear the thought of going home for three days without having seen her, he had arranged to take her to lunch.

'Not yet,' he said, revolving his coffee cup on its saucer. Her hand was resting on the table next to her cup and he reached over to brush his fingers against it. She gave him a warning look, alarmed by a public meeting, let alone a reckless gesture. But he only grinned. They were in a dark corner of a restaurant whose discretion could be relied on and he was so delighted to be with her that he felt immune to danger.

'There's a private view at the Tate next Wednesday,' he said. She nodded. 'Are you going?' he asked her. She looked at him ruefully, understanding his plans.

'I might,' she said, not intending to tease him but genuinely undecided. He reached across the table again, this time grasping her hand decisively so that she jumped. 'Meet me there,' he said in a low imperative voice. He would not let go of her hand and she could not struggle without drawing attention to themselves. 'All right,' she whispered desperately. He released her then and smiled happily knowing that he could now endure the weekend. Priscilla looked at her watch. 'It's after half-past three,' she said. He nodded resignedly and sat back in his chair to look for the waiter.

They left the restaurant and walked toward the Strand. She

started to turn towards Charing Cross tube station but he caught her arm and said, 'Come and have a little walk by the river.' It was a beautiful day, brightly sunny and unseasonably warm. To refuse a walk by the river would have seemed churlish. They crossed over the Embankment and he went to lean against the wall overlooking the river, summoning her with a gesture of his head to stand beside him. She was wearing a thin blouse because of the early hot spell and when he brushed against her arm, he could feel its familiar shape under the sleeve. She faced the river, leaning her elbows on the wall and he turned sideways to watch her. Speaking very quietly although the traffic noise made it inconceivable for them to be overheard, he said, 'I'm going to miss you dreadfully this weekend.' She turned then to look at him but said nothing. He had almost given up expecting her to return his protestations of affection knowing that such utterances would have struck her as more disloyal to her husband than even their physical relationship. The fact that she gave in to him sexually appeased his vanity, but he was continually wounded by her aloofness. Seeing his reaction to her silence, she was caught between remorse, and annoyance that he should feel entitled to make emotional demands on her. A police launch churned noisily down the river and she watched it disappear with its frothing wake under Waterloo Bridge.

'What are you doing this weekend?' he asked, for no particular reason except a vague desire to have at least some hold on her existence while he was gone.

'Not much, really,' she said. 'Julian's away until Monday.' She said it casually, as if the fact could be of no significance to him but he winced, finding the thought of the wasted time while she was on her own almost unbearable. 'Damn,' he muttered. 'I wish to hell I didn't have to go up this weekend.'

Irritated by his assumption that any time in which her husband was absent, should rightfully belong to him, Priscilla moved away and said, 'I must get back,' in her professional, distancing voice. Stung, he reached out to stop her going. The apprehension in his face gave her misgivings and she added more gently, 'You'd better be off as well. It's getting late.' He looked at her for a further moment as if he were memorizing her face and then said, 'I'll ring you at the gallery on Monday.' She nodded and then turned and walked hurriedly away.

★ ★ ★

Fitzjohn could be heard shouting all the way through to reception. His secretary, Clare, ran to him from her office. Nigel Hedding, the *News*'s political columnist, who was standing in reception, grinned at Freddie Clemens, the features editor. 'Oooh, we are working ourselves into a state,' he said in a camp falsetto. Freddie chuckled abstractedly, concentrating on the fastidious folding of his breast pocket handkerchief.

'He's so frightfully excited about it all,' Hedding went on. 'Nearly wet himself when the call came through from Osgood's office.'

'It's something of a coup,' Freddie murmured, 'something of a coup.' He was gazing out of the large window at the view over London. As the sky darkened, the river below them became a black velvet ribbon between two necklaces of lights.

'Will they talk business tonight, that's the question, or just have a beano at our expense so that Fitz can play the wheeler-dealer.'

Freddie gave a warning look to stop Nigel's ruminations as Harry Fitzjohn bustled out of his office. He was beaming now, recovered from whatever the setback was that had provoked his outburst. Clare hovered near him like a nurse. Margaret Crouch from the Lifestyle page and Keith Inshaw, the industrial correspondent, came through from the corridor.

'Oh, *very* nice,' Nigel gushed approvingly at Margaret's cream silk dress. She was heavily made up and had obviously had her hair done for the occasion. She wore her Special Night Out appearance like a rather discomfiting fancy dress costume. Her nervous smile in response to the unaccustomed compliment made Nigel slightly ashamed. More kindly he said, 'You do look very nice.' Clare, glancing at Margaret's dumpy figure encased in cream silk, wondered how she would cope with being seated next to Alistair Thurston whose occasional appearances in the office she still recalled with a slight catch in her throat.

Harry was at his most ebullient, unable to stand still for nervous excitement. This dinner to which all the interested parties in a possible coalition were invited, had achieved a higher rate of acceptance than he had dared to hope. The ultimate triumph was that Gerald Osgood, ex-Minister of the present government who had fallen out rather spectacularly with Number Ten and resigned, had agreed to come. If any Tory was likely to be, as the leader writers said, a standard bearer for moderate Conservatism in some future realignment, it was Osgood. A few damp junior members of the front bench would be here, the most influential Social Democrats along with their advisers, and a handful of Labour right wingers. To fill out the party and conceal its purpose, there were staff from the *News* and an assortment of guests chosen for their capacity to be amusing from London's habitual backlist of socializers. Pre-dinner drinks arrangements were divided between two venues. The more select guest list – players rather than spectators – were invited to meet in the editor's office. The rest had been advised to go directly to the dining suite where drinks would be served at the bar. The growing contingent from the paper were beginning to fill the reception area of the editor's suite making a respectable crowd before the first outsiders arrived. Clare looked at her watch. It was ten minutes past seven. She was beginning to feel out of place in her daytime jumper and skirt. It was only necessary to make one or two final checks on arrangements with catering staff before she could meet her graphic designer boyfriend downstairs in the studio and leave for their favourite Indian restaurant.

One of the stewards, white coated and sleek haired, was preparing a table to act as an impromptu bar in Harry's office. Polished glasses were set in rows alongside a bucket of ice and a plate of lemon slices while Harry radiated anxious approval like a child watching his birthday tea being laid out. There was a small flurry of heightened excitement as the first official visitors arrived. The room was beginning to reverberate with the noisy exuberance of people who were accustomed to commanding a good deal of individual attention. A very tall dark haired man with dissipated good looks moved through the throng with more self-contained poise than most.

'Psst,' Nigel hissed, close to Margaret's ear. 'That's your dining partner tonight. The Heart Throb of the Front Bench.'

Alistair Thurston moved past them without a glance, his eyes searching for interlocutors worth pursuing. Margaret watched him with the hopelessness of an unattached fifty-year-old woman. 'I look forward to that,' she said with game lasciviousness. Nigel winked at her, made slightly cruel by the gin he was consuming with reckless speed, 'Watch out. He can charm the knickers off any red-blooded female.' Margaret laughed robustly choosing to regard Nigel's remark as straightforward ribaldry. Thurston by this time had impacted with Christopher Haileywood, a junior Treasury minister, and Osgood, and they were deep in Westminster tittle tattle. It was ten minutes to eight before Harry began the migration toward the dining suite where their entrance into the larger gathering was ceremonial enough to make it clear that there had been a party within a party. Filtering into this wider company, the individual members of the favoured group each rapidly became the centre of an attentive circle. The crowd of people ossified for a few moments then, with a centrifugal surge, reshaped itself as those most sought after attempted to circulate. Finally, the steward moved among them with a polite suggestion that they might seat themselves for dinner. A moment's hesitation as they concluded present conversations, milled inconclusively, and then with a more concerted decisiveness, merged toward the dining room where the stewards waited to conduct them to their places.

Thurston found his seat, smiled with vague pleasantness at Margaret and skimmed the room with his eyes, able now to survey precisely who was here. When Harry took his place in the centre of the u-shaped table with Osgood on his right and Lady Steen, wife of the *News*'s owner on his left, they all sat down. Alistair found that he had the Social Democratic spokesman for defence on his left for the helpfulness of which he silently thanked Fitzjohn. The meal began with a crab terrine. Thurston, feeling the necessity to despatch the less important of his dining neighbours, devoted the first course to Margaret. He made polite enquiries about her job on the *News*, explored with decent interest the topics to which the Lifestyle page devoted itself – designer artefacts for a middle market audience – and held himself in reserve for the serious conversation which would come later. Even though his charm was reduced to a vestigial civility when faced with an unattractive woman, it was sufficient to animate Margaret's thoughts for weeks to come. The evening as far as she was concerned, was a great success.

They went on to duck a l'orange and a good claret. Alistair, with a movement of his shoulders, gently swung his attention toward the Social Democrat on his other side. William Harris smiled. 'You're having a good week,' he opened accommodatingly. Thurston grinned. 'Not bad,' he admitted. 'Not bad.' At Tuesday's Question Time, he had resoundingly trounced the Labour Environment spokesman in an exchange about nuclear waste, catching him out both on his factual information and the logic of his argument. Since his nimble recovery from the Housing Green Paper débâcle, he had been surefootedly regaining ground.

'Poor Freeman,' Harris lamented sardonically, referring to the Labour Environment spokeskman. 'He can't seem to get it right.'

'It's difficult,' Thurston said wryly, 'to defend an unintelligible position.'

Harris smirked. 'Well, they've all got that problem, haven't they? At least some of them manage to do their homework.'

'He's an innocent Freeman, that's the trouble,' Thurston said. 'He can actually manage to believe six impossible things before breakfast.'

Harris shook his head sadly. 'Don't know how they keep it up. Demographically they're finished. They're going to be marginalized into a minor regional heresy.'

'Political Druids,' Alistair concurred, 'in alliance with the middle class guilt vote in the South and the London fringe lunatics.'

'That's what you call a Broad Church.'

'Your lot,' Thurston ventured, 'are starting to mop up the middle class guilties, of course.'

Harris winced. 'It's the middle class thing we've got to overcome.'

Thurston shrugged. 'There are a lot of them about these days.'

'But it looks too smug. The Party for People Who Are Doing Very Nicely Thank You but Still Have a Conscience.'

'What you need, of course,' Thurston said pointedly, 'is a bit of grit.'

'As in grit-your-teeth-and-face-up-to-reality?'

'Something like that.'

'Pull your socks up, no one owes you a living, we help those who help themselves and hope God helps the rest.'

Thurston smiled. 'You can't get away from it, old boy. It's what people want – personal liberty and economic self-determination.'

Harris sighed and contemplated the remains of duck skeleton which lay on his plate. 'I want to have it all,' he said in childlike self-parody. 'Compassion and puritanism, altruism and privacy – the two sides of the British political temperament.'

'Not forgetting,' Thurston added, as if it were a shopping list, 'an independent nuclear deterrent.'

The plates were being cleared and the interruptions which ensued allowed Harris's eye to be caught by the news editor of the *News* on his left. Alistair was abandoned to Margaret over the pudding, her warmth enhanced by the stewards' assiduous refilling of glasses.

After Fitzjohn had proposed the loyal toast and made a tactfully circumspect speech of welcome, Osgood as unofficial guest of honour delivered a very funny impromptu address, the butt of most of his anecdotes being the present government. Finishing with a swipe at 'Victorian values', he pointed out that from the perspective of his lineage, the Victorians were the original spivs. 'But then,' he commented drily, 'it doesn't do to go on about that sort of thing these days. We're all suburbanites now.' He sat down to laughter and applause.

They all stood then to retire to the suite's lounge for coffee. The banter had increased in jocularity, the party more noisily relaxed in its mellow later stages. This was a further opportunity to change conversational partners and Thurston found himself sought out by Fitzjohn who seemed ecstatic but then he had been looking immensely pleased with himself much of the time lately. Thurston had heard rumours of Fitzjohn's young and beautiful girlfriend and found himself becoming catty in response to Harry's palpable sense of wellbeing.

'You're looking terribly well these days,' he said slyly, fingering Harry's lapel. Harry grinned broadly. 'Second adolescence,' he said with an extravagant wink. Alistair was tempted to say, *Don't wear yourself out*, but instead he smiled kindly, reflecting on the fact that he too would gloat if he dared. To distract himself from the temptation, he turned to Osgood who was standing next to him with Camilla Wolsey, easily the best looking woman in the room. She welcomed Alistair with her eyes and they immediately fell into the mildly playful repartee of a man and a woman who know that they are in the same sexual league. Thurston, Osgood and Fitzjohn encircled her, competing gamely for her attention but it was Alistair at whom she directed her gaze. When he had fingered her earring on the pretext of admiring it, Camilla's husband, Alex, appeared at her side drawing her away apologetically to meet someone. Alistair, recognizing this move as the compliment to himself that it was, underlined it by saying, 'Keeping a close eye . . .' Osgood smiled and murmured, 'Quite right, too.'

* * *

At half-past one in the morning, Alistair lay fully dressed on top of his bed, still too stimulated by the evening to sleep. Images of the party floated across his mind and settled on Harry Fitzjohn's slightly reddened, exuberant face which made an open secret of his private delights. Suddenly irritated beyond endurance, Alistair picked up the telephone by his bed and dialled Priscilla's home number. It rang three times before she answered and her voice was clearly barely awake.

'It's me,' he said simply.

'Alistair?' she was shocked into alertness.

'Sorry,' he said, knowing what an outrage this call was but sufficiently drunk not to care. He knew that Julian was away. Priscilla had spent the previous afternoon in bed with him, freed for three days by Julian's trip to Aberdeen.

'What's happened?' she asked, obviously terrified by a call at this hour.

'Nothing's happened,' he said soothingly. 'I just wanted to

hear your voice.' She was silent for a moment, then she came back with real anger. 'You fool,' she whispered furiously. 'You mustn't do this.'

'I know,' he said, now really contrite. 'I'm sorry. Were you asleep?'

'Of course I was,' she snapped.

'Are you still in bed?'

'Yes,' she answered, perplexed by the question. 'We have a phone in the bedroom.'

'Good,' he said softly. 'I want to talk to you while you're lying in bed. It's almost like being with you.'

Priscilla shut her eyes, appalled by the enormity of what he was doing and by her own longing to submit to his mood. His voice, here in her own bedroom, in Julian's bedroom, was like a dream of being chased and unable to run. He was telling her how much he wanted her, how he wished he could make love to her over the telephone. She lay against her own pillow with her eyes shut listening to him as she did when he was lying beside her. He had invaded her last sanctuary and she could not find the will to repel him. He paused and said, 'Speak to me,' and she was suddenly able to summon up the words. 'Stop it, Alistair. Don't ever do this again.' Then she put the phone down.

But the room was alive with him now, the bed contaminated by his presence. She drew her knees up and hugged herself protectively. Her breasts felt warm against her arms and her bowels were stirring expectantly. She pressed her hands to her belly to quieten her arousal but her flesh jumped at her own touch. Then she cried, as much from physical frustration as from fear.

* * *

Debbie pressed the bell beside the glass door of the editor's suite. The porter inside glanced up at her from his seat behind an array of telephones and then the buzzer sounded unlocking the door. She pushed her way through, smiling at the porter who said, 'If you'll just take a seat, Miss. He's still in a meeting.'

She went to sit on one of the three sofas which were arranged at right angles around a chrome and glass coffee table, sinking comfortably down into the upholstery. There was a murmuring of office activity from the hive of rooms leading off this reception area, the low reverberations of electric typewriters, telephones ringing, the rolling of filing cabinet drawers, muted voices. Looking round her at the chocolate brown walls, dotted with white framed photographs of political figures, she felt a small thrill of possession. The fact that the man who was at the centre of this belonged, in some sense, to her, made this place her own as well, as if his power were embodied in the hold that she had over him. She sat in a self-consciously relaxed posture, an insider, at home in these intimidating surroundings. Wearing a jersey dress which she had bought that morning because she knew that its tactility would appeal to Harry, she sat largely ignored by the staff who trotted through the reception area importantly, depositing and collecting messages from the porter's desk. She caught the eye of a familiar looking youngish man on such an errand and smiled in her engaging way. He responded in kind, if a bit abstractedly.

'Clive,' called a voice from the corridor, and the man turned abruptly. 'I've got Nigel on the phone,' the voice went on. 'He can do Wednesday but not Monday.'

'Oh, Christ,' the man in reception responded. 'Hold on to him. Got to check my diary.' And he sprinted away down the corridor.

There was a commotion then at the far end of the reception area. The party from the editor's office was emerging with eruptions of the loud laughter and uninhibited boisterousness of powerful men. 'Don't push him too hard, Fitz. He's a bugger when he feels threatened,' bellowed a tall man with steel-grey hair and a ruddy complexion. There was a robust but inaudible shout in reply from inside the office which provoked roars of hilarity. The grey-haired man's face became more flushed with rowdiness as he called back, 'Now, now Jeremy. We're not having that.'

Harry suddenly appeared in the midst of this jovial group. In this assembly of politicians and their advisers, he was almost unrecognizably altered in manner. His private personality to which Debbie had become accustomed, was now so affectionate and unportentious that she had almost forgotten the imposingness of his professional persona. He was engaged in a heated but good humoured contretemps with one of the party, a younger man with curly black hair and horn-rimmed glasses. 'We can hammer it out when the time comes, Ted,' Harry was saying. 'Don't fret about it.'

'We can dot the i's then,' the man called Ted replied. 'But we've got to get the big ones sorted now.' The grey-haired man with the red face clapped his hand on to Ted's shoulder. 'Come on now. Rome wasn't built in a day and neither is a coalition.' Ted subsided unhappily and Harry gave him a cheerful pat on the back. Then he turned and saw Debbie sitting on the sofa watching him. His gregariousness became more energetic as he exulted in the pivotal influence of his position and Debbie was acute enough to know that he was showing off to her. As his coterie dispersed with noisy exuberance, she stood to approach him. He turned to her, smiling broadly, elated by the meeting and his usual delight in her presence. Walking over to her quickly, he took hold of her arm with frank possessiveness and a number of his departing guests smiled at him with genial envy. Braying final goodbyes, the meeting group were gone and Harry led her back into the office. Made shy by the formidableness of this incarnation in which she had caught him, she was so subdued that it made him look at her. She smiled at him, almost appeasing, and it pleased her to see his daunting façade drop away. 'How are you?' he asked, with his usual gentleness.

'I'm fine,' she said, still slightly abashed. He took her hand with his most kindly and protective air and led her to the seats by the window of his large office. The leather upholstered chairs were arranged in a ragged semicircle after the meeting, and the detritus of purposeful conviviality – full ashtrays, and glasses which held melting ice and slices of lemon – cluttered the coffee table.

'What have you got there?' he asked, indicating the folder she was carrying.

'It's the Bond Street piece,' she said, slightly crestfallen.

'Oh, of course,' he said, the quickness of his response being a kind of apology. In the excitement of his political intrigues, he had forgotten that she had arranged to bring in her latest feature for his approval. 'Let's have a look then,' he said, taking it from her. 'Did you speak to all the people you'd hoped?' he asked, with punctilious recollection of the details.

She nodded. 'I spent an hour with Webber, and D'Arcy gave me a very good interview.' It was a profile of the most influential Bond Street art dealers. Priscilla Burford had been very helpful with background information and Debbie felt that the piece she had put together would please all the participants. Harry was glancing through the typescript. 'You haven't said anything about their more unsavoury activities, have you? They're very quick on the trigger with libel writs.'

'Oh no,' she said. 'It's all very much as they wanted it said.' He smiled and handed the typescript back to her, obviously unable to give it any real concentration. 'It's fine,' he said. 'Give it to Freddie and we'll get it in the pipeline.'

Mildly piqued by his continuing distraction, she decided to talk about the only thing which was of interest to him at the moment. 'What was your meeting about?' she asked, putting her article back into its folder. His face became more animated as he replied. 'That was a little horsetrading over the next government.'

'After the election, you mean?'

He nodded and smiled mischievously. 'But they can't be sure of the result,' she objected.

'No,' he agreed. 'This is just preparing the ground.' He laughed and added, 'They're just sorting out what they'll say to the voters as opposed to what they'll say to each other.'

'Won't all the deals be made after the election?' she asked.

'The final ones will depend on the details of the result. But if everyone gets sounded out in advance, it will save a lot of time.'

She went thoughtfully quiet and he leant back to look at her attentively for the first time. Recognizing the softening in his facial expression, she reached over and touched his hand. 'Do you want me to arrange for some photographs to go with this?' she asked, indicating the folder. 'That would be a very good idea,' he said, engrossed in watching the movements of her mouth. He looked at his watch then. 'It's nearly six,' he said. 'I can get away a bit after eight. Shall we go for a meal?'

'Okay,' she said happily. 'Shall I come back here for you?'

He nodded yes and took hold of her hand to give it a squeeze. She smiled, then leant forward to kiss him lightly on the mouth. He held her arms, wanting to kiss her properly but she slipped out of his grasp and stood up.

'See you later,' she promised as she turned to leave, satisfied now that he would spend the next hours thinking impatiently of her.

* * *

Priscilla had fallen asleep lying on her stomach with her face turned away from him. It was nearly ten o'clock and Alistair did not want her to rush away so he leant over her, kissing her between the shoulder blades to wake her. She opened her eyes instantly, having been in only a light doze, and turned to face him. 'What time is it?' she asked, immediately worried that she had stayed later than she had planned.

'Not yet ten,' he said soothingly. 'No hurry.'

She raised herself on one arm to look across him at the bedside clock as if she did not trust his word and he let her check the time before pulling her down on top of him. She kissed him and then dropped down to lie on him, her breasts compressed softly against his chest. She seemed so tranquil that he ventured in a gently teasing voice, 'You're not sorry that you came now, are you?' She did not reply, allowing him his small gloating reprisal for the difficult time she had given him. A week before she had, once again but more definitively this time, told him that she would not see him any more. He had subdued her reluctance repeatedly with his confident assurances and his fervent persistence, but this last declaration of hers had been of a different order and not until he had been reduced to frantic desperation had she relented. The fact that her husband was away had helped his cause. She always resisted him most strenuously when she knew that it would mean returning to face Julian immediately afterwards. He kissed the top of her head and whispered, 'Spend the night here.'

She sat up, pulled a weary face and gave him a soft, playful punch in the stomach, in exasperation at his request. He caught her and held her before she could move away. 'Please,' he said, 'Ring the au pair and say that you're spending the night with a friend.' She sighed at his incomprehension of the realities of her life. Deciding to make some attempt at making him see her dilemma, she said archly, 'And not be there when the children wake up tomorrow . . . and then when Julian gets home, they can mention the fact that Mummy wasn't there on Wednesday morning and he will want to know where I was, and if I say "At a friend's", he'll want to know which friend's . . .'

Alistair knew that he was beaten and gave in resignedly. Pulling her down on to his chest again, he said, 'You'll just have to come with me when I make a trip out of London. I'm sure the gallery can arrange some excuse for you to go to Manchester or Wales for a couple of days.' This was a familiar refrain. He said repeatedly that he wanted to be able to spend more than a few hours with her, and she balked insistently at his demands, terrified not only of discovery but of being drawn into an even deeper involvement than the present one which she pushed constantly to the margin of her life. Her continued refusal to enter into the affair with unreserved enthusiasm kept him on tenterhooks. However inconvenient or dangerous it might prove to be, he wanted her to fall in love with him, to be as dependent on his attentions as he knew she could be if she would only relax her guard. To his intense irritation, her resistance so challenged him that his feeling for her was becoming more and more obsessive. Where the first fascination might well have been declining, the affair now beginning to pass a peak which would eventually bring its end within sight, he was instead growing incensed by his failure to win her over. He could not leave her alone, being pushed closer to recklessness than he had ever permitted himself to be before.

She made no reply to his suggestion, knowing that it was pointless to argue, only resolving to herself that there would be no such trip. His arms were around her waist and he turned over suddenly, pulling her underneath him. He looked down at her, pinning her arms by her sides and clamping his legs around her so that she could not move. 'I'm going to keep you right here,' he said. She smiled, eased one of her hands in between their bodies and slid it along his pelvis. As she had known that he would, he reacted by arching his back with a shock of arousal and she was able to push him away in his moment of agonized excitement. She slipped out of her side of the bed as he reached out furiously to grab hold of her but she put herself quickly out of reach. He dropped on to his back groaning with what sounded like real suffering, then said in a voice whose self-pity was only half-joking, 'You are terribly cruel to me.' But she had gone off to the bathroom which adjoined the guest bedroom and he subdued his frustration, knowing that she was now resolved to leave.

He brought her some coffee as he always did before she went home and made her sit on the bed to drink it. He sat next to her, sipping a brandy and soda to calm himself. It annoyed him that she was so eager to go and for a moment he considered making some physical move which would make her want to stay. But although seducing her again could be done, her responses being well-known enough to him by now, it would in the end only serve to make her feel more threatened. Consideration for her feelings was more in his interests than not, even if it meant submitting his pride and his body to some discomfort. He kissed her goodbye before they left the bedroom and was pleased that she accepted his stated intention to ring her the next day without protest.

★ ★ ★

Thurston did not arrive at his office until half-past eleven on that Monday, having spent the weekend in Yorkshire and driven back to London early in the morning. He was surprised, and rather pleased, to find a message waiting for him saying that he was to ring Priscilla that evening at a Hertfordshire telephone number. The first thing that occurred to him was that she had succeeded in getting away from London for a few days and was inviting him to meet her. He was able to leave the Ministry by seven and was not required at the House until the division at ten, so he drove himself home rather than summon a car. It was nearly half-past seven when he reached Cadogan Square and while his man prepared a small supper for him, he went upstairs to ring Priscilla from the bedroom.

An older woman's voice answered with a recitation of the number, as people in the country still tended to do. He asked with formal politeness, since he had no idea whom he was addressing, to speak to Mrs Burford. The voice asked for his name and he gave it, sensing a barely perceptible fluster at the other end of the telephone when he did so. Then the voice said, with stiff politeness, 'Just a moment, please.' Silence for several minutes, then Priscilla sounding so strained that he knew instantly that there had been a catastrophe.

'Alistair?'

'Yes,' he said, his voice already tense with expectation. She paused for only a fraction of a second then said in a stark, tight voice, 'Julian's found out.'

Fortunately, he was sitting down. He was sure that he would have collapsed had he been standing. He stammered incredulously, 'How – how could he have found out?' wanting to disbelieve it.

'He saw one of your letters,' she said, with an unmistakable note of accusation. Responding to her tone as much as to the words, he snapped, 'What? Why did you let... Why didn't you destroy them?' She did not answer this directly but simply said, 'The last note you sent to the gallery got mixed up with papers I was taking home.'

Priscilla,

I miss you desperately. If I haven't got through to you on the phone by tomorrow, I shall come to the gallery. We had so little time last Tuesday. I must see you before I go to Yorks. for the weekend.

Love,

A.

He shut his eyes, recalling with horrific clarity the wording of that frantic note. Then he asked, his voice desolately quiet, 'What is he going to do?' Her voice broke and although she kept herself under control, he knew that she was crying. 'He's going to file for a divorce. At least, that's what he says.'

'On what grounds?' Alistair asked, the panic beginning to roar in his ears.

'Adultery,' she said quietly, knowing that she was telling him now what it was he really needed to know. 'He says that he'll name you as co-respondent.' The floor seemed to rise up at him and he gripped the edge of the bed. He tried to speak but his voice failed. Taking a deep breath, he tried again: 'How much did you tell him?' She seemed rather taken aback by this question, her words when they came, expressing her surprise, 'I told him everything . . . as much as there was to tell. There was no point in trying to hide anything.' She did not say that Alistair's note had said it all, had been so unambiguously incriminating that there was little left for her to do but fill in the details.

'Is he really going to go through with it? Can't you persuade him to see sense?' He would not accept this. It could not be happening. Surely the situation had to be salvageable. She had been so concerned about any risk to her marriage that there must have been a great deal between them. Julian would get over it and take her back.

'I don't know,' she said bleakly. Then she added, becoming tearful again, 'He was beside himself. He found the note on Saturday morning and I had to send the kids out for the day. He went on and on, wanting to know how much the gallery had known about it . . . I came up here on Sunday.'

'Where are you?'

'At my parents'.' She had driven there on Sunday with two confused but largely oblivious children, leaving Julian silently adamant. 'Have you spoken to him since?' Alistair asked her, his mind still racing but becoming more coherent.

'He won't speak to me but my father is going to London to see him tomorrow.'

'Will that have any effect, do you think?'

She sighed. 'I don't know. My father is very sane and Julian has always respected him. He may be able to get somewhere.'

Comforting himself as well as her, Alistair said, 'He'll have calmed down by then. He should be more amenable.' Then he added, 'Don't worry.' She said nothing for a moment, then, 'I'll ring you when I know anything more.'

'All right,' he replied. 'Ring me at home tomorrow evening.' Then she rang off.

As soon as he put the telephone down he stood up as if it were going to be possible to take some action. His legs began to shake as he took a step and he dropped back down to the edge of the bed, covering his face with his hands. He was sweating profusely although he felt ice cold and for a moment, he was completely incapacitated, unable even to take the decision to lie down. But then, forcing himself into sense, he did lie down and immediately felt better. The relief of escaping that sickening debilitation freed his mind to function more rationally. The worst thing was not knowing. He wanted to ask for advice, to marshal his friends and contacts, confide in his wife on whose support he would be dependent; but if it were all a false alarm, if Julian allowed himself to be calmed and won round, then it would be best to have told no one. Could he bear living with this uncertainty in silence for however many days or weeks it took for the situation to clarify itself? He tormented himself with possible courses of action for a further half-hour, running through the permutations of people whom he could rely on and consult. By the time he had pulled himself together sufficiently to go downstairs and eat the meal which had been prepared for him, he had decided to tell only Harvey Wynne – who was a personal friend as well being an absolutely reliable political ally. Having settled this in his mind as an effective provisional step, he was then able to eat, shower and shave before returning to the House with some degree of self-possession.

It rained all day on Tuesday. The feeling of unnatural coldness which had overtaken him during Priscilla's telephone call had remained, and with the dampness of the weather permeating his body, he felt as though he were locked in some dank cellar. And as well, his throat ached from the stress which constricted it. Harvey was sticking very close to him. His obvious concern made Alistair realize how alarmingly distraught he must appear. Their conversation the previous night had drawn him out of his private hysteria. Harvey, fully aware of the situation's danger, had nonetheless maintained a cool decisiveness which was exactly what Alistair had required. As soon as he had seen him at the House, Wynne had known that there was something really wrong.

'I'm in a bit of a mess,' Alistair had begun apologetically. Sensing that this was not one of Thurston's usual bleats about his love life, Wynne had waited for him to go on. 'Been caught out,' Alistair had said in such a terrified hush that there was no way that this could be taken with anything other than complete seriousness.

'What do you mean?' Wynne had asked gravely, thinking at first that there was a pregnancy. Alistair ran his hands over his face and said, 'Her husband's found out. He's talking about a divorce.'

'Naming you?' Harvey asked, quietly appalled. Alistair nodded, unable to say anything more.

'Jesus,' Harvey murmured. Then, seeing that Alistair was close to complete disintegration, he had summoned up his most imperturbable manner and asked, 'Does Kate know?' Alistair had shaken his head. 'I've only just heard. Priscilla phoned me from her parents'.'

'She's left home and gone to her parents'?' Wynne had asked then. Thurston nodded. That, Harvey knew, although he did not say so to Thurston, was an unwise thing for her to have done. To have left the marital home would count against her in a divorce court. Alistair, getting his breath back, explained to Harvey that there was still some hope for the marriage to be saved. Harvey's advice then reiterated exactly Alistair's own view: say nothing to anyone until it was absolutely beyond doubt that a divorce action was unavoidable. Alistair asked Harvey to come back to Cadogan Square on Tuesday evening. They could have dinner at Alistair's house and then spend the evening waiting for Priscilla to ring with news of her father's meeting with Julian, returning to the House together for the division at ten.

★ ★ ★

In his own home, away from any public sighting, Alistair gave in to his state of nervous collapse. Harvey's sympathy for him, in his dreadful agitation, overcame any embarrassment he might otherwise have felt at seeing another man in such a frankly disabled emotional condition.

'Sit down,' he said gently. 'You're going to make yourself ill.'

They were in Thurston's drawing room, Harvey sitting on one of the cream sofas, Alistair pacing fretfully with his arms folded across his chest. He had barely eaten any of the very pleasant food that had been set out for them informally in the breakfast room and now he looked so deathly pale that it made Wynne wish that he were free to summon Thurston's wife.

Alistair sat down obediently, made passive by the paralysis of his own will. More than anything, it was this sense that his fate was out of his hands which was incapacitating him. Then at ten minutes past nine, the telephone rang and Thurston went rigid. 'Shall I?' Harvey asked, moving toward the telephone, but Alistair shook his head and leapt across the room.

'Hello,' he said, his voice rushed and tense.

'Alistair?'

'Yes,' he answered, and then had the civility to add, 'How are you?' She ignored that and said simply, 'My father saw Julian today.'

'And?'

She paused and he could tell that the news was not good. 'He spent all day with him,' she went on, her voice distant and collected as if she had already exhausted all her expressions of emotion. 'He's absolutely set on a divorce.' She paused. 'And he is going to name you.' Wynne saw Alistair reach up and grab the doorjamb for support. Priscilla's voice was going on: 'He's told me to get a solicitor because he'll be using our old one. My father told him that he wouldn't act as a go-between, that Julian must come and talk to me. So he's coming to see us at the weekend.'

Alistair's voice sounded dry and strangled when he replied, 'When he sees you, you'll be able to talk ...' He could summon up, even in his present state, a mental picture of Priscilla which made it seem absurd that any man would not relent on seeing her. She did not reply and he said, his sense of honourable behaviour not lost, 'You can see my solicitors. I'll take care of it.' Her voice was impatient and arch when she replied. 'I don't think that would be wise. We shouldn't really have any more contact at all. I'll see to it that you find out everything you need to know.' Then she rang off, leaving him stunned. For a horrible moment, he thought he was going to be sick. Standing very still with his eyes shut, he felt Harvey's hand on his arm and allowed himself to be led back to the sofa. Harvey asked him nothing, just poured out a large brandy and brought it to him.

The details of Julian's relentless outpourings to her father: how humiliated he was by this apparently long-running affair in which her work colleagues had been complicit, his amazement at her ability to come home to her children after these illicit meetings, the inconceivability of his ever living with her again when the face of her lover would confront him regularly on television, caused Priscilla to feel that Alistair's hopes of 'making him see sense' were faintly ludicrous. What counted as 'seeing sense' to someone like Thurston – taking these things in one's stride and not allowing them to touch the basic foundations of one's life and position – was not part of Julian's mental landscape. For him, as also for her, life as it was and life as it appeared were largely the same thing. His professional existence, which was the real definition of himself, carried with it a certain kind of package in which his domestic situation played a crucial role. The way he saw himself, the way he functioned in the world and the way he conducted his personal life, were all of a piece. To have discovered that there was, in this picture that he had constructed of success and security, another dimension altogether of anarchic, clandestine forces was undermining not only to his marriage but to his understanding of how the world was. It was unthinkable for him to accept the continuance of their life together because the knowledge he had now gained rendered his own judgement of what was real, untrustworthy. It was absolutely necessary to be rid of this devastating reminder of those things which had been at large in his most intimate surroundings but had somehow escaped his notice. Priscilla, without having heard Julian's righteous arguments to her father and without his even having articulated these views to himself, understood all this and knew that their marriage was over.

* * *

They sat drinking tea in the breakfast room, Alistair, Harvey Wynne and Ted Drucker, PPS to the Secretary of State for the Environment. The first necessary steps had been taken, Alistair having sought an immediate confidential meeting with his Secretary of State to inform him of the scandal which was about to hit, and to offer his resignation. The Minister, of a different political complexion from Alistair, being further to the right of the party, nevertheless harboured no ill will toward him. In fact, he thought Alistair an exceptionally talented young man whose abilities helped to cover the bets of the party for the future. He had shaken his head over Alistair's confession and murmured, not without affection, that he was a silly ass to have landed in this predicament, but he thought it might be possible to avoid resignation. The Cabinet Secretary and the Prime Minister's private office would have to be informed instantly and the situation discussed. His advice in the meantime was for Alistair to summon his wife to his side and present an impregnably respectable face to the world.

Alistair had already done exactly that on Wednesday morning, the telephone call to Yorkshire having been mercifully brief. He had begun by asking Kate to come to London straightaway, in a voice which was so constrained and urgent that she responded with wary alarm, 'What is it, Alistair?'

'I'm in something of a mess,' he had answered, his tone subdued by embarrassment and apology. She was silent for a few seconds, then she said, 'Is anybody pregnant?'

'No.'

'Worse?'

'In a sense, I suppose it is.'

'My God, Alistair, what's happened?'

'It looks,' he had replied hoarsely, 'as if I'm going to be named in a divorce action.'

To his eternal gratitude, she made no comment on this at all, but simply said with cool reserve, 'I'll come down tomorrow. Do you want Tommy to come with me?'

'No,' he had said quickly, relieved that the horrendous message was now imparted and received, 'there's no need for that. Will you drive yourself?'

'No, I'll get Barry to take me.'

'All right,' he had said then, his voice imploringly grateful and warm. 'I'll see you tomorrow.' It was a manner she knew well. Alistair was never more endearing than when he was laid low. The fact that he turned to her at every major crisis in his life, that he was, in fact, utterly dependent on her emotionally whenever things failed to go well for him, had sustained her through many of the most trying moments of their marriage. When his anxiety was compounded by guilt, his efforts to please her were almost excessively lavish. Quite unconsciously, she anticipated the coming weeks with a small degree of pleasurable satisfaction although by far the greater emotion was fear for his professional future.

They were waiting for her arrival now in Cadogan Square, Alistair fretfully impatient, feeling with some magical sense of trust that her presence would enable him to deal even with the intolerable waiting which had to be endured. Word had gone to the Cabinet Office and to Number Ten and, in the way that these things do, had travelled through the House and rippled out into the circles of press and political hangers-on. It was discussed in the wine bars of Fleet Street and the pubs of Gray's Inn but, because of the libel laws, not a word of it could be printed until it was official fact rather than gossip. Thus, the open secrets of public life may or may not eventually find their way into the great organs of information which present the citizenry with political reality.

Thurston's man appeared at the breakfast room door and said, in the sombre attentive tone which he had adopted since the crisis had begun, 'I think Mrs Thurston's car is here, sir.'

All three men rose expectantly, Wynne and Drucker preparing to absent themselves as soon as Kate arrived. Thurston could hear Kate being admitted through the front door, acknowledging his man's muted pleasantries, then coming down the corridor past the dining room. When she came into the room, Wynne and Drucker both smiled at her and she exchanged civil greetings with them before they slipped out to continue their supportive vigil in the drawing room. Then she looked at Alistair directly for the first time. He looked worse than she had expected, almost sick with anxiety. He met her eyes with a gaze so painfully trepidatious that she was instantly beyond any need for retribution. He stood with formal politeness while she approached him. Giving him a few seconds of torment while she paused, she then reached out her hand to touch his arm and said kindly, 'I think you'd better sit down.' His knees nearly buckled with relief and he did sit down, taking hold of the hand with which she had touched him.

'Have you heard anything more?' she asked, her voice competently assured. He shook his head. 'We're waiting for some word from Number Ten.' He did not add that one of the things that Downing Street was waiting to hear was how his wife would respond. If she were prepared to support him and smooth it over, there was a much better prospect that they would see him through it. Alistair suspected that, at this moment, Ted was telephoning the Downing Street private office from the drawing room, to say that Kate was now on the scene. There were a great many questions which she wanted to ask about the details of this situation but Alistair looked so fragile that an interrogation at this point would have seemed inhuman. Instead, she asked, 'Have you had anything to eat today?' knowing that his appetite tended to fail under stress.

He shook his head. 'I don't think I could keep anything down.' She squeezed the fingers of his hand which was still holding hers. He had had no proper sleep for three days and suddenly, with his tension eased, he was overwhelmed by exhaustion. 'Why don't you lie down for a while,' Kate suggested. 'You look pretty dreadful.' With her here to look after things, he felt that it might actually be possible to rest. 'Will you wake me if there's anything?' he asked. She nodded and stood up. They went upstairs to their own bedroom, a room to which he had never taken any other woman, and he dropped down on to the bed in collapse. 'Do you want anything?' she asked, about to leave him to sleep. He shook his head but then reached out quickly to grab her hand. 'Stay with me for a bit,' he said, keeping his eyes shut. Without replying, she sat down in the wing chair a few feet from the bed and remained there until he had fallen asleep.

* * *

Malvern lit Robert Lucas's cigar and then his own. 'Rotten luck, isn't it?' Lucas shook his head in despairing agreement. Bevis went on, 'He can never get past a pretty face.' Lucas said peevishly, 'Why couldn't he get himself a secretary or an assistant? Doesn't he like single girls?'

Bevis shrugged. 'I think he prefers them more mature. There's something maternal about married women.'

Lucas, the Prime Minister's PPS, would not be cajoled into understanding. 'Stupid sod. He can be mothered by his own wife.' Bevis smiled. 'He's terribly romantic, that's the thing. Falls in love like a schoolgirl.' Lucas grunted, 'Well, he may just have been ruined by his romantic nature.' Bevis winced theatrically. The whole point of this meeting he had contrived was to sound out those closest to Number Ten and engage their sympathies for Alistair. If Lucas's relentless disapproval was anything to go by, the PM's circle were not taking it well.

'We don't have to get too frantically puritanical about this, do we?' Bevis asked with distaste. 'Not puritanism,' Lucas shook his head reprovingly. 'I'm not advocating puritanism. Just prudence.'

'Well,' Bevis said with a sweet smile, 'we all get imprudent from time to time, don't we? Can't lose a good man who's at the beginning of his career just because he lost his head over somebody else's wife.'

Lucas was appropriately chastened. 'Who the hell is this chap, anyway?'

'The husband?'

Lucas nodded over the whisky with which Malvern had been plying him.

'Absolutely no idea. Some little man in computers, I think,' Bevis replied dismissively. Then he added irritably, 'Very tedious of him to get so nasty. The whole thing would have been over in a couple of months.'

'Alistair must have been pushing things if he managed to be found out,' Lucas said, returning to his previous unforgiving tone.

'I don't know,' Bevis said, 'it may have been her doing. She's an ambitious girl. Perhaps she thought she could land Alistair if she exposed the thing.'

'Is that what she's like?' Lucas asked, brightening with interest. Bevis shrugged. 'I don't really know her. Met her a few times. Very charming, clever lady. Certainly stage managed the Macmasters business very smartly.' Lucas was looking intrigued. If Thurston had been trapped by a social climbing adventuress, his position could seem morally salvageable. Bevis saw the light in Lucas's eye and refilled his glass. Then he said, 'Poor Alistair. He can be a bit naive about these things. He'd be better off sticking to his own circle.'

* * *

The Secretary of State for the Environment, David Lambert, sat in his office drinking tea with his PPS, Ted Drucker, and his Permanent Secretary. 'He's an awfully talented chap,' Drucker was saying regretfully. Lambert nodded sadly. 'I'm not at all sure that we can save him, though. Once the popular press get it . . .' he sighed. 'And in these unstable times Number Ten isn't going to be happy.' The Permanent Secretary, who had always found Thurston a particularly amiable and competent Junior Minister, had had lunch that day with the Cabinet Secretary who had also not been optimistic about Thurston's future but whose goodwill, already considerable, had been enhanced by the Permanent Secretary's favourable report on him.

'What are the odds, do you think?' Drucker asked.

'Six to four against, I'd say,' Lambert replied.

'His political excursions going to count against?'

Lambert shrugged. 'Don't think so, really. Whether they admit it or not, the leadership knows that somebody has to make some overtures in case the worst happens. He's been very discreet about that.'

Drucker smiled. 'Pity he wasn't quite so discreet about everything else.' They all chuckled quietly. For all their concern, there was nonetheless something of the elation that front line soldiers are reputed to feel when their mates are shot down beside them.

'Have you spoken to him today?' the Permanent Secretary asked Lambert. The Minister shook his head. 'Nothing to tell him yet.'

'Poor devil.' Drucker said. 'He must be sitting by the phone.' Thurston had taken the last two days off sick from the Ministry, everyone having agreed that he should remain diplomatically out of sight until a decision was reached about his fate.

'Saw him in the House last night,' Drucker went on, referring to Alistair's appearance for the division at ten which had had a three line whip and could not, therefore, be avoided. 'He looked like death.'

'Oh, dear,' the Permanent Secretary murmured with real

compassion, and the grief in his voice transported them all from their slightly flippant despondency to genuine sadness.

* * *

At half-past eight that evening, Harvey Wynne settled himself on the red plush of a bench at the Quill and Ink, to wait for Harry Fitzjohn. The deep intonations of male conversation reverberated around him, enfolding him in a stolidly reassuring sense of normality after the day he had spent in Cadogan Square. The Thurstons had coped admirably with the constant flow of visitors who had arrived to confer and offer their support, but Alistair's sickening anxiety was close enough to the surface to give the atmosphere the unreal self-containment of a devastating crisis, like a hospital ward or a home which awaits a death. Wynne had had the same sense when he left the house, of surprise that life outside was still continuing, as he remembered from his vigil during his father's last illness.

It was at Alistair's behest that he had arranged this meeting with Fitzjohn, in the mellow recesses of a pub whose mahogany panelling and red carpets had witnessed many a judicious conclave. He had bought a bottle of very good claret and it stood open now on the table to breathe, in anticipation of Fitzjohn's arrival. A steady stream of men filed through the door, complacently engrossed in each other's companionship. What few women there were, were of a superior caste, the Quill and Ink harbouring no shrieking typists or giggling colonials. Finally, noticeable even in this prepossessing company, Fitzjohn entered, paused for a moment to locate Harvey and then walked toward him with the demeanour of a man who knows that his arrival is not without portent. A number of heads turned to offer covertly interested glances as he walked past. Harvey stood to shake his hand and then touched Harry's arm to offer the seat beside him. He poured out two glasses of his generous offering and opened the conversation with civil enquiries about Harry's health and that of his newspaper, whose financial condition had given rise recently for concern. Harry gave reassuring answers on both points and then asked with frank sympathy after Alistair.

Harvey shrugged philosophically. 'As well as can be expected, as they say.'

'It's a mess, isn't it?' Harry asked rhetorically, with a depth of concern which confirmed Alistair's prediction that Fitzjohn would be inclined toward helpfulness.

Wynne nodded. 'Awful pity. The worst of it is,' he elaborated, 'this is his moment. The wets are about to inherit the earth. If he has to retreat in disgrace now, he might just miss his chance.' Harry was entirely aware of the political truth that it was not sufficient to be the right person if you were not available at the right time. If the crucial historical point were missed for any reason – personal misfortune, bad judgement, failure of nerve – one might slip like thousands of others into the backdrop of obscurity. He drank some more of Harvey's excellent wine and permitted himself, from his position of emotional and professional security, a moment of vicarious depression over Thurston's calamity. Then he turned to Wynne and said, 'How is Number Ten taking it?'

'Saying nowt at the moment. He's not close to them, of course, but they think he's a bright lad and he's well-liked everywhere. They don't want to lose him if they can avoid it.'

'His wife is around now, isn't she?'

'Oh yes. Been there from the moment it broke. Good sound lady. She won't let him down.'

Fitzjohn nodded slowly. Wynne was silent, allowing Harry as much time for meditation as he required. 'Who is this woman, anyway?' Harry asked then, having forgotten that he had actually once met Priscilla.

Wynne sighed. 'A publicist from an art gallery. She was setting up an arrangement for a big buyer her gallery deals with to give his collection to the nation. She caught Alistair's eye, and brought off a very good deal for her gallery.'

Harry smiled. 'She was obviously prepared to go to great lengths to bring it off.'

'Yes,' Wynne said ruefully. 'Would that she hadn't been quite so dedicated.'

Harry drew in a resolute breath and said, 'He can't go down over this. Some clever girl wants to clinch a deal and he ends up on the political scrap heap.'

'It's not good enough, is it?' Wynne agreed, picking up Harry's determination. Then, feeling sufficiently confident about Harry's sympathies, he said carefully. 'Much depends on how your lot play it, of course.' In addition to the fact that Harry was not one to become censorious about other men's peccadilloes, he had an investment in the saving of Thurston's future in terms of his own political judgement and machinations. But the clamouring imperatives of even the middle-brow press required that scandal could not be ignored. Thurston's affair would be a hot Fleet Street property which no amount of circumspection could deflect from its disastrous course. His mind clearly running through the possibilities, Harry ventured, 'Can't the husband be talked round? At least to changing the grounds?' Wynne breathed out an exasperated noise. 'Nobody knows him. He's just some little chap who takes it all terribly seriously and wants his pound of flesh.'

'But hasn't it occurred to him that the publicity will be humiliating for him? And what about children – are there any?'

'I think so,' Harvey replied, knowing that there were because Alistair had told him so but, for some reason, unwilling to dwell on that fact. 'Well,' Harry argued, 'they'll be dragged into this as well. For their sakes, he should keep the whole thing as quiet as possible.'

'You'd have thought so, wouldn't you?' Wynne agreed. 'But who's going to persuade him of all this?'

Harry subsided again to reflect and finish off the last of the wine. 'I'll get another bottle,' Harvey said, standing up. Harry caught his arm and said with a puckish smile, 'Don't. I have a very pleasant evening planned. I don't want to be completely immobilized.' The thought of Debbie waiting for him at his flat, of the unproblematic nature of the arrangements in his own life, sent a flush of self-satisfied pleasure through him, making him contented and restlessly lustful at the same time. From the invigorating happiness of his own excitement, his generosity toward Alistair was enhanced. 'I think,' he said with conviction, 'that we might be able to bring some pressure.'

Wynne looked up, his face registering unashamed relish. 'How?' he asked, genuinely curious. Harry said quietly, 'If enough of the reporters who are hanging around ask sufficiently hostile questions, he might get the idea that it wouldn't be wise to sling too much mud.'

Harvey smiled. He would be able to return to Alistair with as favourable a report as they could have hoped.

There seemed to be no lights on in the flat when he first came in and he had a bad moment of alarm and disappointment. But then he heard the faint sound of electronic speech and realized that Debbie was watching the portable television in the bedroom. Unable to think of any more delightful place to find her, he opened the bedroom door. She was lying on the bed, gazing half-heartedly at the screen which prattled at the foot of the bed. His appearance took her by surprise, the sound of his arrival having been obscured by the noise of the television and she looked up startled as he came in. Her face immediately suffused with happiness and she reached for the remote control switch to turn off the television. Her cotton skirt was hitched up above her knees and as she sat up to greet him, she pulled it down in an unconsciously demure gesture. He stood over her, almost overwhelmed by sensual pleasure, hardly needing even to touch her. She smiled and said, 'You're late.'

'I know,' he said. 'I'm sorry.' Then she reached up to take hold of his hand and with that contact, the abstract fascination broke and he was taken over by his more usual specific desire. He slipped out of his jacket and removed his tie before stretching out on the bed next to her, wishing that they could simply undress and make love without further preliminaries. But their relationship was not so superficial as that and he did not want to hurt her with callous urgency. She turned on her side to face him and he said, by way of explanation of his lateness, 'Had to have an emergency meeting with an MP. Somebody's got himself in a spot of bother.'

She looked at him with curious interest. Unable to resist impressing her, he went on, 'Have to extricate a junior minister from a mess.'

'Who's that?' she asked, laying her hand on his stomach. He reached up to hold it there, loving the sensation of stirring warmth that it sent through him.

'Alistair Thurston. Always been something of a lad. This

time he's really come unstuck. Been carrying on with a lady whose husband has turned very nasty.'

'Thurston?' Debbie said in surprise.

'Yes. Do you know who he is?'

'I've met him,' she said. The seriousness of her tone made him look at her. For an anxious moment, he wondered if she might ever have had anything to do with Thurston herself. Then she asked, 'Who's the woman?' He could not at first recall the details but then he said, 'She works for an art gallery. Don't know the name.'

Debbie looked appalled. 'My God,' she said.

'What's the matter?'

'She's a friend of mine. I didn't realize that she'd got that involved with him.'

Disconcerted by Debbie's inside knowledge of a situation which he had enjoyed being privy to, he asked with new respect, 'Who is she?'

'She's a publicist for the Houghton Gallery.' Then she turned back and poked him affectionately in the stomach. 'I was with her, the night I first met you.' He smiled and pulled her to him. 'I'm afraid I can't remember anything esle about that night except meeting you.' He pushed her down gently and kissed her in a way which was obviously a serious prelude to intercourse. Instead of taking his cue and undressing immediately as she normally would have done, she drew back after the kiss and said, 'What's happened? Has Priscilla's husband found out?'

'I'll tell you all about it,' he said with pointed intentness, 'later.' She made a playful face and got up from the bed to take off her clothes.

* * *

Julian had spoken to their solicitor on Thursday. The conversation had been grimly awkward. Paul Meadows had known them as a couple for ten years, having handled the purchase of both of the houses they had owned during their married life. Not quite a personal friend, he had been more than a voice on the end of a telephone. Drawing up their wills, dealing with the legalities when Julian's father had died, he had necessarily become involved in their family concerns. Julian ringing him to announce that he wanted to file for a divorce was so startling that Paul had at first assumed that he was joking. When the seriousness of the request was put beyond doubt, Paul's manner was transformed almost immediately into professional discretion. The familiar warmth of his opening greeting to Julian withdrew into distant politeness. Had he not been, in his great stress, relieved by this cool, impersonal tone, Julian might have sensed a note of disapproval. But his own businesslike terseness matched Paul's respones and, in a ten-minute conversation, they were able to exchange the preliminary information that was required. Being an only child with a very infirm mother as his one surviving close relation, he had no family to whom he felt obliged to communicate the news of his marriage's end.

Krista had stayed on in the house for the time being. She knew that Priscilla was going to her parents' for some while and Julian had advised her that it would probably be best for her to contact the agency and seek another post. So far as he knew, she had done this but she continued to clean the house while he was at work and to make herself as unobtrusive as possible when he was at home. He had maintained an apparent calm in his outward behaviour since Priscilla's father's visit during which he had therapeutically given vent to his outrage. His father-in-law had responded to Julian's indignation with sympathy but had implored him, for the sake of the children, to think very carefully about the step he was taking. Julian had replied that it was Priscilla who needed to be reminded of her obligations to the children.

That evening, after his father-in-law had gone, he had had a telephone call from Beth of all people. Completely unaware of the apocalyptic events in his household, she had asked to speak to Priscilla.

'She isn't here,' he had replied, so curtly that Beth had realized the irregularity of the situation immediately. 'Do you know when she'll be back?' she had asked carefully.

'No,' Julian had said abruptly. Then, in a more normal, redressing voice, 'I'm not sure. She's at her parents.' Thinking that there was some crisis which involved perhaps, the health of one of Priscilla's parents, Beth said, 'Oh, is anything wrong? Can I help with the kids?'

'The kids are with her.' The cold finality of Julian's answer had closed off any further enquiries and Beth murmured a goodbye before ringing off. It took another day before she could piece together from various sources the story of what had actually happened to cause Priscilla's departure.

In the last two days there had been a development which was more disturbing to his composure than anything that had occurred since the discovery of that note, the image of which still recurred in his dreams. He had begun receiving telephone calls from newspapers, some from tabloid features departments offering to buy his story for large sums of money, others from individual reporters hounding him for interviews. He had, of course, refused to respond to any of these but the questions were becoming nastier, some even suggesting that there might be 'facts about his marriage' which could be revealed by other people if he himself was not prepared to reply. One journalist had made it clear that he knew a great deal about Julian – where he worked, how frequently he travelled abroad and where he stayed, implying that an exposé of his own life was planned which would involve talking to his employers and colleagues. Reporters and photographers had appeared at his front door and lingered there until he had summoned the police. It was humiliating to him to admit that he was frightened by all this. The office had become aware that something was going on because they were getting odd telephone calls and requests for information about him. He had, very briefly, been tempted to accept an offer for his story from one of the papers because it involved protection from all other press approaches as part of the arrangement. The anxiety created by this harassment channelled itself readily into anger against Priscilla who had brought this upon him. Persecution was enhancing his sense of his own innocence. The more he felt himself victimized, the greater was his desire for retribution if only to right what was beginning to feel like a cosmic injustice.

On Saturday morning, he prepared to drive to Radlett to make the promised visit to Priscilla and the children. It did not occur to him to wonder how he would feel on seeing her for the first time since she had left – he was not the sort of person who attempted to anticipate or examine his own feelings overly much – but he was looking forward to seeing Emily and Jaimie whom he had missed. Busying himself with washing the car and ironing a fresh shirt, he had avoided thinking any discomfiting thoughts. At half-past eleven, the telephone rang.

'Mr Burford?' a pleasant female voice asked to his 'hello'.

'Yes.'

'This is Helen Miller from the *Daily News*. I believe a colleague of mine spoke to you yesterday.' Her voice was sweet and appeasing.

'I told your colleague that I had nothing to say to the press,' he replied, growing pompous in his agitation.

'I realize that, Mr Burford,' she went on with apologetic courtesy. 'It's just that we are preparing a story and we wanted to clarify one point.' Before he could refuse, she carried on, 'Is it the case that there is a young woman living at your house with you now?'

For a moment, he was so shocked that his mind went blank. Then the penny dropped. 'That's the au pair,' he blurted, in a tone of startled protestation.

'I see,' the voice said with grateful warmth, 'so your au pair *has* gone on living with you after your wife has left.' He was so taken aback that he could say nothing. A further fraction of a second and the voice said, 'Thank you, Mr Burford,' and rang off.

* * *

Priscilla was in the back garden when he arrived, sitting in one of the floral sun chairs which were grouped around a white wrought iron table on the patio. Her parents' house was a large, detached mock Tudor affair built between the wars with a garage and summer room added on more recently at the back. Emily was sitting on Priscilla's lap having a story read to her, her brown curly hair just visible above Priscilla's shoulder as she sat with her back to him. His mother-in-law had shown him through the house, a bit tearful but obviously determined not to interfere. She had vanished immediately when Julian walked through the French doors into the garden.

Jamie saw him first and leapt up from his sitting position at the edge of the fish pond with a delighted shriek. The sight of his son running towards him across the lawn made Julian suddenly distraught. The overwhelming anger of the last week had extinguished any sense of loss but now, faced with the sight of his family in the idyllic sunshine of this garden, he was weak with sadness. Emily scrambled down from Priscilla's lap and raced after her brother to leap into Julian's arms. He lifted Emily on to his shoulders and Jaimie trotted along next to them, chattering happily about the bird's nest he had found that morning. Priscilla stood up and turned to face Julian but he occupied himself with the children, refusing to meet her eyes. Emily, squealing with pleasure from astride Julian's shoulders, leaned forward and peered into his face. 'Are you going to take us home, Daddy?' she asked expectantly. They had often come to stay with their grandparents when he was on trips abroad and always, on those occasions, he would come to see them on his return and they would all go home together. Julian did not answer her question, distracting her by swinging her downwards in the sudden, thrilling way that she loved. She collapsed in a giggling heap at his feet and Julian smiled at her. Priscilla smiled as well but when she caught Julian's eye, he looked away. She did not know whether he wished her to send the children in so that they could talk. She waited for him to indicate what it was he wanted, afraid to make any move that would annoy him. But he continued to ignore her, talking to Jaimie and allowing Emily to pull him to the ground and climb happily over him. Watching him play so delightedly with the children, Priscilla was encouraged to think that he might be having doubts about his decision. When finally, he sent Jaimie in to the house to get the bird's nest in which he took so much pride and despatched Emily to her grandmother, she turned to him expectantly. Breathless from his exertions on the grass with Emily, he asked with simple coldness, 'Have you got a solicitor?'

Slightly stunned, she said, 'I've spoken to my parents' solicitor.' This was not precisely true. She had agreed with her father that she would consult his solicitor for advice but had refrained from actually doing so in the hope that it might not, in the end, be necessary.

'Ask him to contact Paul next week,' Julian said tersely. Then he turned back to Jaimie who was trotting up to him, bird's nest gripped in his hands. A further half-hour passed before Priscilla's mother ventured tentatively out the back door to ask if they would like some lunch. Julian shook his head quickly and said, 'I thought I'd take these two out for lunch and a little drive.' He looked at Priscilla then to whom he had not spoken since their one earlier exchange. 'All right?' he asked with respectful civility. She nodded silently. This visit was not, she realized definitively, any attempt at reconciliation. He was already the estranged husband, visiting his children at the weekend. Jaimie and Emily clambered happily into the back seat of Julian's car, thrilled with this unexpected treat. When they had turned the corner of the drive, Priscilla rushed upstairs to the spare bedroom where she had been sleeping. Her mother came in quietly ten minutes later and sat with her while she cried, stroking her hair as she had done when Priscilla was a child.

★ ★ ★

'Christ, they are giving him an easy ride, aren't they?' Ted Drucker said as he finished reading The *Times* leader. He was sitting with Harvey Wynne, poring over the newspaper coverage of Thurston's love affair. With the filing of Julian's divorce action, the miasma of gossip and anecdote which had hung over Fleet Street had been licensed for public release. It was, of course, front page material for the tabloids. The *Sun* had 'Minister in Love Triangle with Art Gallery Girl', with a photograph of a smiling Alistair Thurston, taken at a party the previous year. Its story related, in simple terms, an account of the Macmasters Collection arrangement and how beneficial it had been to the art gallery for which Priscilla Burford worked. The *Mail* put 'Thurston Named in Divorce Action' on the front page. The story on page two recounted the role that Priscilla had played in negotiations with the Ministry to achieve an agreement on the Macmasters Collection. It pointed out as well, what a competent and respected junior minister Thurston was and quoted his Secretary of State, Lambert, as saying that he was 'one of the most able younger members of the government.' The *Mirror* splashed 'Tory Minister in Divorce Scandal' on the first page and followed it with a history of Thurston's career to date, pointing out that he was one of the most liberal and progressive voices on the Conservative Front Bench.

It was the quality press which had particularly provoked Drucker's observation. The story appeared on page two of *The Times*, a small item containing the basic facts of the divorce action in the first paragraph and a judiciously disinterested retelling of the Macmasters Collection story in the second. Priscilla's function as publicist for the gallery and her initiation of discussions on the presentation of the collection to the nation were carefully noted. This was followed up by a leading article, the third in the leader column, in which *The Times* gravely observed that 'Government ministers are always prey to the ambitious – those who would exploit contacts with political power for their own ends . . . ' Without once mentioning Priscilla's name, the piece implied that Thurston, who was described as 'an immense asset to the Government and to the political future of the country', had been culpable only in his naiveté.

The *Daily Telegraph* story, on page three, gave the facts of the divorce and carried on with a series of quotes from Cabinet Ministers and Conservative Party officials, praising in benevolent terms the abilities and character of Alistair Thurston. Mention was made of the fact that Thurston had offered his resignation but that no decision had yet been made as to whether it would be accepted. It was thought that opinion among Tory constituency parties was being canvassed.

On the second page of the *Guardian* was the story titled, 'Tory Wet Named in Divorce', which concentrated on Thurston's 'courageous' record of leftish opposition to the Government's more draconian measures. One of its political correspondents had a feature on the leader page which covered the issue of doomed Tory wets more broadly, commenting on how many of their careers had come to untimely ends, and coming close to insinuating that the Thurston scandal was part of some sinister right wing Conservative plot to discredit liberal Tory politicians.

Harvey sniggered as he dropped the *Guardian* back on to the pile of newspapers, 'With any luck, he should survive it.'

Ted was reading the *Express*. He glanced up. 'Do you know,' he said, 'that one of the Diaries actually said that Thurston's problem was that he was too attractive to women for his own good. It made it sound as if he'd been carried off against his will.'

In his own office, Bevis Malvern was also scouring the press reports. Sitting with him was his PPS, Dickie Fielding.

'Not too bad, is it?' Dickie said, fanning himself with a folded copy of the *Mail*. July had brought heat and humidity of sub-tropical proportions. Distant rumblings of thunder promised eventual relief but for now, even open windows did little to shift the oppressive stillness.

'Not bad at all,' Bevis agreed. 'Have to see what the Sundays say, of course. They'll have had time to digest it by then.'

'But this is only the opening round,' Dickie warned. 'The shit really hits the fan during the actual divorce hearing.'

'If it comes to that.'

'What do you mean?'

'There's still some hope that the wronged husband,' he pronounced the phrase with ringing melodrama, 'will have a change of heart – or at least not kick up too much mud.'

'*Is* there?' Dickie smiled, entering into the gossip with some enjoyment. Bevis winked. 'People are trying to make it clear to him that it would not be wise.'

'I should think so,' Dickie said. 'Who could possibly have to gain from that?'

'Quite,' Bevis agreed righteously.

* * *

'I think she's gone off with him,' Beth said conspiratorially.

'No, she hasn't,' Rachel almost snapped at her. 'She's with her parents. I spoke to her last night.' She was alarmed and disgusted at the intemperate speculation which was reverberating around the neighbourhood.

'How is she?' Beth asked defensively, hearing Rachel's annoyance.

'Not very happy.'

Beth was silent for a moment, chastened by Rachel's gravity. Then she asked, 'How are the kids?' Rachel sighed. 'They still have no idea what's going on. They can't really understand why they've left school before the end of term. Jaimie is most concerned about the insect project he was working on in class, apparently.'

'She hasn't told them anything?'

'What can you tell a seven- and a four-year-old?' Rachel asked irritably.

'Well, she's going to have to say something eventually, isn't she?'

'Maybe not. They might patch things up yet.'

Beth seemed more shocked by this idea than anything that had been discussed before. 'Do you think so? From what the papers say, it doesn't seem likely.'

'The papers,' Rachel replied, incensed, 'are full of crap.'

'Maybe they are,' Beth rallied. 'But it's hard to imagine any man taking a woman back after everything that's been in print.'

Rachel was finding this conversation more and more infuriating partly, she knew, because Beth's views were probably close to those of most people. If even Priscilla's friends could talk in such lurid terms about the situation, it was appalling to think what the world at large must be making of it.

'I'm going to have to go, Beth. Peter's just got back.' Rachel's voice was resigned now and not unfriendly.

'Okay. When you speak to Priscilla again, give her my love and ask her if there's anything I can do.' Beth was conciliatory as well, not wanting to fall out with Rachel who was the pivotal member of their local circle.

'I will,' Rachel said and then she rang off because Peter really had just arrived back. She raised her eyes heavenward at him in tribulation. He looked at her quizzically.

'Beth,' she said in explanation. He smiled. 'Don't take her too seriously.' His voice was mild and imperturbable.

'It isn't just her,' Rachel said. He waited for her to go on, helping himself to a can of lager from the fridge. With a gesture, he asked her if she wanted one as well and she nodded. They walked from the brick pier of the kitchen to the sofa and sat down together. She poured the beer into glasses and said, 'What's worrying is that everyone must be thinking pretty much the same thing. Beth is just tactless enough to say it. What chance has Julian got to think rationally?'

Peter sipped his lager and gazed thoughtfully up through the open void above him to the roof rafters. 'He's pretty level-headed,' he commented blandly. Rachel held her glass against her face enjoying the coldness of it in the muggy heat. 'From what Priscilla says,' Rachel countered, 'he's not being very level-headed at the moment.' Peter said nothing for a minute, then, 'Well, she would feel that, wouldn't she?'

'What do you mean?' Rachel asked, completely taken aback. Peter drank some more of his lager, wanting to forestall what he knew was going to be a serious disagreement. 'Obviously,' he began slowly, 'Priscilla would prefer it if Julian weren't so adamant. But that's not to say that he's behaving irrationally from his point of view.'

Rachel was stunned not so much by his words as by his moral neutrality. It had never occurred to her to question the fact that the breakup of the Burfords' marriage was sad and unnecessary. 'But how could it be rational?' she asked. The shock in her voice was open and uncontentious. Peter did not look at her as he replied evenly, 'She *was* rather spectacularly unfaithful to him.'

Rachel was at a loss to reply to this. It was not often in their marriage that they found themselves on completely different wavelengths. 'But they have two children ... ' she began.

'All the more reason for her to have behaved herself,' he responded, with a quickness that made Rachel realize that this opinion was well-formulated. His reaction was much more fundamental than she would ever have expected, as if the infidelity of any woman were so personally threatening to him as a man, that Priscilla was automatically cut off from any sympathetic consideration.

'If it were Julian who'd had an affair – with a secretary, say,' Rachel said with measured preciseness, 'would you think that Priscilla should chuck him out without a second thought?'

He still did not look at her as he answered. 'Probably.'

'That doesn't sound very rational to me.' He said nothing so she went on. 'It sounds vindictive and intolerant. You don't throw away everything that you've had together because one person's made a mistake.'

'It was a long series of mistakes,' he said wryly. Rachel

sighed in exasperation. He turned to face her at last. 'Look,' he said. 'It wasn't one little slip from the straight and narrow. She had a long-running affair. He wrote her love letters. How do you think Julian's going to feel knowing that that was going on under his nose?'

'I don't know,' she said quietly. 'How is he going to feel?' She asked it honestly, bowing to his male authority.

'Like a fool,' Peter said simply. Rachel sat still for a moment, eyes downcast. Then she said, 'There are worse things to be than a fool.'

'I know,' Peter replied kindly.

'I was going to ask you,' she said then, 'if you'd talk to him and try to persuade him to be reasonable.' He looked at her, sorry to have let her down, to have put such distance between them. 'I can't interfere,' he said softly. 'It's his life.'

'And hers.'

He sighed philosophically. 'If he wants to talk,' he pointed out in his more usual patient voice, 'I'm sure he knows he can come to us.'

* * *

It took some persuading before Simon would agree to contact Priscilla. He was touchingly protective about her, adamant that she would not want to see anyone. But Debbie was insistent, her argument resting on the conviction that she might be one of the few people in a position to help. He rang the Hertfordshire number at last, while Debbie stood over him.

'Priscilla,' he began apologetically when he had got through to her. 'Debbie Ackerman is here and she wants *very much* to speak to you.' There was a pause and then he handed the receiver over to Debbie with a reserve which clearly implied that it was against his better judgement.

'Priscilla?' Debbie said into the telephone. Then, 'Look, I've got to see you about all this shit you're getting from the press . . . no, honestly, I think there's something I can do. Please, I won't do anything without your permission but just let me come and talk to you.' Her urgent concern was so apparent that Priscilla was obviously moved.

'Great,' Debbie said. 'How do I get there? . . . How about

tomorrow afternoon ... can I phone you from the station? ... Fine. See you tomorrow.'

As she rang off, she smiled at Simon. There was no hint of triumph in her face, only delight that she had succeeded and could now accomplish what she had planned. He smiled back at her, won over as well by her sincerity. 'Do you really think you can do anything?' he asked hopefully. Her grin became mischievous. 'Well, I have got some cards to play that aren't available to other people.' Thinking of Harry turning himself inside out to please her, she added, 'I can use my influence.'

* * *

Radlett station was set deep in greenery at this time of year. The rural tranquillity was stunning, coming up so quickly on the train out of London. It was not unlike, Debbie thought, the more affluent commuter suburbs of Connecticut or upstate New York. A cream-coloured Rover pulled up outside and Debbie, recognizing Priscilla at the wheel, came out to meet it. Priscilla reached across to open the passenger door and then pulled away as soon as Debbie had scrambled in, obviously in a hurry to get out of even this minimal degree of public view. Debbie looked across at her as she drove. She was drawn and unmade up, her hair pulled back tightly away from her face. For all that, her profile was still striking. She had the sort of looks, Debbie reflected, which ought to have made her very successful in dealing with men. That she had ended up in this mess was an extraordinary mishap.

'It's just down here,' Priscilla said, aware that she had not spoken since Debbie had got into the car. She had regretted inviting Debbie almost immediately on putting the telephone down the day before. The appeal had seemed so earnest that Priscilla had consented but now the incongruity of Debbie's presence here seemed bizarre and futile. The fixities of her parents' home and assumptions made an almost unfathomable contrast with this oddly transient American girl. What possible use this meeting could serve, she could not imagine.

Debbie smiled as they pulled into the drive 'It's like a Connecticut house,' she said

'Is it?' Priscilla asked, surprised that anything in this setting should seem familiar to Debbie. They got out of the car and Priscilla motioned for Debbie to follow her. They walked around the house to the garden where Emily sat with Priscilla's mother. Jaimie rushed up to Priscilla as she appeared around the corner of the house 'Mum,' he called excitedly, 'look what I've got.' Priscilla and Debbie both stopped to see. He held up his cupped hands and then opened them a crack very slowly. In the cavern made by his curved palms sat a Red Admiral butterfly with its wings tightly closed. It was impossible to tell whether it was terrified into stillness or lulled to sleep by the warm darkness of Jaimie's hands.

'Oh Jaimie, let it go,' Priscilla said.

'It's okay,' he protested. 'I'm not hurting him.' He was indeed holding the butterfly with as much gentleness as could possibly be expected from a seven-year-old boy.

'You mustn't hold him too long,' Debbie said. 'Butterflies have very short lives. If you stop him flying for an hour, it's like a year would be to us.'

'Really?' Jaimie asked incredulously. Debbie nodded. 'What's just an afternoon to you could be a quarter of his life.' Jaimie seemed very impressed by this. 'I'll let him go soon,' he promised gravely. Priscilla's mother turned toward them and Debbie smiled at her with a well brought up diffidence which made Priscilla realize that this kind of family life was not so far from Debbie's own experience as she might have thought. 'This is Debbie Ackerman,' Priscilla said and her mother greeted Debbie, responding to her as the familiar kind of nice girl which she appeared to be. Priscilla then ushered her inside, obviously having arranged for her mother to keep the children occupied in the garden while they talked. They entered through the back door into a large kitchen whose walls were lined with oak cupboards. Priscilla asked her if she would like a cold drink and they agreed on orange juice, taking their glasses with them into the living room. Priscilla shut the door behind them and then sat down on a loam coloured sofa. The mahogany coffee table in front of them held a stack of small cork mats and Priscilla took one of them to put under her glass. Debbie immediately did the same, recalling her own mother's rules about placing glasses on polished wood. Debbie leaned back against the sofa then and asked, 'How are you?' Her voice was so solicitous that Priscilla, for the first time, was grateful for her visit. She drew away from the question. 'I'm coping,' she said.

Deciding to come straight to the point, Debbie said, 'What I want you to do is to tell me your side of the story as an interview.' Priscilla looked alarmed as Debbie had expected that she would. She went on purposefully, 'You must tell it as it was. If you don't say anything, the papers will just gang up on you. They don't like people who won't speak to them.' Priscilla was beginning to seem receptive so Debbie persevered, 'If you give the interview to me, I can see to it that it says exactly what you want. I'll let you read it before I hand it in.' Priscilla was not protesting so Debbie added, 'It's worth a try,' meaning *nothing could be worse than things as they are.*

'I suppose you're right,' Priscilla said finally, unable to hold out against Debbie's persuasiveness. Debbie touched her hand in a gesture of open sympathy and then reached down to the canvas bag she had brought to extract a small, ringbound notebook and a pen. Priscilla looked at them as if she were seeing the surgical instruments with which her leg was to be amputated. Debbie smiled. 'Come on,' she said gently. 'It's only me.' Priscilla smiled as well. She took a determined breath and asked, 'Where do I start?'

'When you first met him,' Debbie answered decisively.

Priscilla shut her eyes as if recalling the whole saga was almost more than she could bear. But then she began, with tentative embarrassment at first but with more fluent detail as she relaxed under Debbie's perceptive attention. For an hour and a half they sat undisturbed while Priscilla recounted the story of her relationship with Alistair Thurston and Debbie patiently took notes. When she reached the point of Julian's discovery of the fatal letter, Priscilla's voice broke and Debbie cut in kindly, 'You don't have to go any further.' Priscilla stopped and pulled herself together with a strenuous act of will. Then, in a calm voice, she said, 'Shall we have some tea?' Debbie nodded and they got up to walk back to the kitchen together.

Priscilla's mother was there. The cotton dress and white sandals that she wore were not unlike the kind of suburban summer uniform of the women in Debbie's family. She had not met anyone of this type in England before, her life here having been confined to circles of cosmopolitan London people who seemed to exist without roots. Priscilla and her mother busied themselves compatibly in the kitchen making tea and slicing a fruit cake to serve with it. They took their cups and plates into the garden because it was such a beautiful day, and the children buzzed around them preventing any continuation of the earlier conversation which had, anyway, pretty much exhausted itself.

'It's a lovely garden,' Debbie said to Priscilla's mother.

'It's a bit parched now,' her mother commented, looking around her complacently. 'But the roses have done very well.' She was still a pretty woman with well-cut grey hair and Priscilla's light blue eyes. 'Your father fed them *devotedly* this year,' she said to Priscilla.

'Have you made a decision about the clematis?' Priscilla asked her.

'*I've* made a decision,' her mother said dryly, 'and I think I shall just do it. He probably won't even notice.' She smiled at Debbie and gazed down to the bottom of the garden. 'I do think that some of those old fruit trees are going to have to go this winter.'

There was something about the calm mundanity of her conversation, the imperturbable pleasantness of her voice, which made Debbie marvel. She could not imagine any American woman, caught up in a public scandal over her daughter's adultery, drinking tea and chatting about the garden.

It was after five when Debbie made a move to leave. Priscilla looked at her watch and said that there would be a train from Radlett station in twenty minutes. As they walked around the house to the car, Debbie said, 'The letters that you mentioned – could I take any of them with me to corroborate the story? I promise I'll return them. I'll take photocopies and send the originals back to you.'

Priscilla smiled ruefully and said, 'You can keep them.'

'No,' Debbie said urgently. 'You keep them. Your divorce lawyer will need to see them. Don't destroy them.' Priscilla nodded, accepting Debbie's advice once again, and then turned back to the house to get Alistair's letters.

* * *

'What have you been up to, then?' Harry asked sweetly as they were seated at a corner table of a restaurant where he took her often. She had told him rather mysteriously over the telephone that she had had a trip into the countryside. She smiled at him and said, 'I was doing an interview.'

'Oh, yes.' He beamed at her indulgently. 'What was that?'

The waiter arrived to take their orders and Debbie accepted the interruption gratefully. She had not decided how to announce her venture to Harry, wanting to choose the optimum moment for prevailing upon him. His attempts to maintain a dignified degree of restraint in the face of her teasing provocations had become an established sexual game for them and she had planned vaguely to make use of the inevitable point in the evening when he would promise her anything. Deciding to hold out for this, she said softly, 'I'll tell you later,' her voice hinting at the more intimate circumstances of a later conversation. He smiled, happy to endure even the impatience which the next few hours entailed. She listened to his account during the meal of his negotiations with the print unions over new technology at the *Daily News* and then, with considerable appreciation, to a funny anecdote about one of his political friends. When they had finished eating and he had got through a bottle of wine, she said, 'I had a letter from an old college friend of mine this morning. She's just arrived in Florence.'

'Really?' he asked pleasantly, the alcohol and her company making him feel comfortably relaxed.

'She's renting an apartment there and wants me to come and stay with her for a while.'

It took a few seconds for what she had said to register on his face. 'You don't want to go, do you?' he asked, his voice taut with apprehension.

She shrugged non-commitally and looked down at her empty coffee cup. 'I don't know really. I've never been to Florence.' She did not look at him but she could feel that he was almost breathless with anxiety. When she glanced up, he was facing straight ahead, avoiding her eyes. Even when she reached over to touch his arm, he did not turn to her. 'I wouldn't go forever,' she said softly.

He said nothing at first, then very quietly, 'I don't want you to go at all.'

She gazed at him but he would not look at her. 'Don't you?' she asked tenderly.

'No,' he said in a cracked voice. She watched him struggling to control his facial expression.

'Well then, I guess I'd better not,' she said fondly, genuinely affected by his reaction. He shut his eyes for a second in relief, then turned to face her. His expression was both adoring and reproachful. 'You are a little minx,' he said.

She was sincerely sorry now. 'I didn't think you'd mind that much.' He made an exasperated face at her as if she were foolish to underestimate his feelings. Then he looked up to call for the bill, eager now to get her home and in to bed in order to expunge the last traces of his sense of abandonment.

* * *

It was only when they were back at the flat that he started to feel more like himself. He began kissing her as soon as they sat down in the living room, dispensing with his usual subtlety almost as a punishment for the scare she had given him. Knowing that he could not be held off for long, she drew away, taking hold of his hands.

'Do you know who I interviewed today?' she said.

'Who?' he asked quickly, not wanting to be pulled for long out of his amorous fog.

'Priscilla Burford.' When he did not respond to the name, his mind still unfocused with sensual preoccupation, she elaborated, 'The woman Alistair Thurston had an affair with.'

'Did you?' he asked, a vague consternation struggling to the surface of his mind.

'She gave me a terrific interview. It will be a great scoop for the *Daily News*. She hasn't told her story to anyone else.' He did not look pleased by this but before he could speak, she leant over to kiss him. Her embrace now was without reserve and it put him beyond the point of making any objection.

* * *

'I think you'd better have a look at this,' Freddie, his Features Editor had said, sounding slightly arch over the telephone. 'Do you want me to send it up?'

'Yes, all right,' Harry agreed, refusing his underling the satisfaction of asking him why. Debbie's article arrived on his desk within minutes and when he had read it, his eyes racing over the copy with professional expertise, he understood what had provoked Freddie's snickering tone. Debbie had, in fifteen-hundred words, pulled the plug out of the warm bath of loyalty in which Thurston's career had been kept afloat. Priscilla's account, so straightforward and unpretentious as to be absolutely convincing, blew to pieces the reassuring concoction of justification to which they had all contributed. For an exhilarating moment, Fitzjohn had the godlike sensation of holding someone's life in his hands. The typescript seemed to be ticking against his fingers. At a word from him, it could become front page copy on tomorrow's *Daily News* and Alistair Thurston's political career would be finished. But the effusion survived so briefly that within seconds he had forgotten that he had ever felt it. It was followed by a more characteristically rational series of decisions. He would ring Freddie and tell him that the story was killed. Then he would contact a few of Thurston's allies to warn them of the potential danger in anyone interviewing Priscilla Burford. Lastly, he would ring Debbie and ask her to come into the office. When Debbie had spoken to him, she knew without any doubt why he was calling her in.

He had already given his instruction to Freddie and spoken to Harvey Wynne and Ted Drucker by the time she arrived at noon. She came into the office and shut the door behind her looking, Harry thought, like a mischievous schoolgirl who had been summoned by the headmaster. Her obvious awareness of what she had done made it easier for him to say what he had to say. He looked at her with rueful irritation, deciding to play the affectionately angry father. 'That was very naughty of you,' he said.

'Was it?' she asked with quiet defiance.

'That piece would finish Thurston.'

She shrugged. 'Maybe it would, but it's the truth.'

This made him defensive and he said, 'It's her version of the truth.' Without a word, Debbie reached for her canvas bag and took a large envelope from it. He watched her with surprised curiosity as she extracted what she had expected it would be necessary to produce at some stage. On photocopied sheets were reproductions of three of Alistair's letters to Priscilla. Debbie set them down on Harry's desk with calm ceremoniousness.

Priscilla,

I must see you. Why won't you return my messages? I'll come to the gallery if you don't ring me by tomorrow.

Alistair

Priscilla,

I don't know how you can be so cruel. Please come to the house on Thursday night. I will send a car to the gallery if you want. I will do anything you want if you will just come to see me. I love you.

A.

And then his last note to her which Julian had found:

Priscilla,

I miss you desperately. If I haven't got through to you on the phone by tomorrow, I shall come to the gallery. We had so little time last Tuesday. I must see you before I go to Yorks. for the weekend.

Love,

A.

There could be no doubt about their authenticity. Two of them were actually written on Ministry of Environment headed notepaper. (*The bloody fool*, Harry thought.) One was signed with Alistair's full Christian name, the others only with an initial, but they were all in the identical rushed, scrawling handwriting which spoke of real desperation. Debbie was watching with patient satisfaction as he read. Without looking at her, he said quietly, 'We can't publish it.'

She was standing in front of his desk and when he glanced up at her she looked dumbstruck with shock. Seeing the expression on her face, he said in appeasing explanation, 'It would wreck his career.'

'He's wrecked her life,' she said simply. He was sitting behind his desk while she still stood. Unsure of whether it was the breach of manners or her stance of accusation which bothered him, he said, 'Sit down, Debbie,' with parental firmness. It seemed to take her a few seconds to realize what he had said, then she turned and sat down in a chair some distance from the desk as if she wanted to escape from the force of his personality. He was becoming annoyed with himself for not being able to contain this situation with his usual authority. The letters, with their embarrassing starkness, had wrongfooted him. His conviction that the article should never see the light of day was unchanged but he now felt himself to be party to something really unsavoury, and Debbie's clear-eyed perception of it made him all the more uneasy.

'There's more at stake,' he said, trying not to sound pompous, 'than his career.' She was familiar enough with his accounts of his own political manoeuvres to know what he meant. But she replied, 'I doubt that the future of the country could hang on one politician.'

Trying another tack, he said, 'What would be accomplished by printing it? Her situation wouldn't be any better and the country would lose a good man.'

'A good man?' she repeated sarcastically.

'A good politician,' he corrected grudgingly.

Debbie sighed and said, 'She's been dragged through the papers as some kind of scheming temptress. Her own husband probably believes it by now. And she isn't like that at all. In fact,' Debbie continued with something like disgust, 'she's an incredible innocent. If she hadn't been, she wouldn't be in this mess.'

Harry was losing patience. He did not want to have to defend his position any longer. 'For Christ's sake, she's a grown woman. She must have known what sort of game she was playing.'

Debbie looked startled. She was hurt and shocked by his tone. 'Never mind her,' she said, staring at him. 'Don't you have any desire to print the truth, for its own sake?'

He smiled sardonically. 'The trouble is that everybody's got a different idea of the truth.'

'So,' she said coolly, 'the truth can be whatever suits you and your friends.'

He was really angry now, undermined as much by her disapproval as by her argument. 'You're very naive about these things,' he snapped. 'You don't understand how things work in this country.'

She smiled then, unperturbed in her detachment. 'I think I see very clearly how they work.' Then she stood up and started to walk toward the door of his office.

'Wait a minute,' he said with the kind of casual authority he would have used with his staff. She waited until he had walked out from behind his desk and come to stand in front of her. With judicious benevolence he said, 'I'll get Thurston over here to read it and see what he has to say.' His stern, patriarchal tone made it clear that he was intending to confront Alistair and dress him down. Even by the standards of their male circle, which permitted a fair amount of latitude, Alistair had behaved badly. Fitzjohn, who had, by his own intervention, saved Alistair's skin, was aware of his private responsibility to upbraid him.

Debbie nodded vaguely, this offer having little significance for her, for whom public truth was more important than private honour. She was unaware of the code which ruled that to be castigated by one's friends was ultimately much more serious than being pilloried by the press. She turned toward the door and Harry caught her arm. 'Why don't you stay for lunch?' he asked, his voice reverting to its normal tenderness. She shook her head and said, 'Have to meet a friend,' and then left so quickly that he was startled by her sudden disappearance.

He returned to his desk and sat down, feeling unsettled and morose, wishing that the scene with her had not ended so badly. Then he rang Thurston's private line at the Ministry and left a message saying that he needed to see him as soon as possible. Half an hour later the Principal Private Secretary telephoned back to say that the Minister was leaving for his constituency at five o'clock and could drop in at the *Daily News* on his way.

* * *

Harry's secretary had gone home by the time Thurston arrived at five-twenty so he was shown in by the porter. Harry stood to greet him, noticing how much better he looked than when they had last met. Alistair was recovering his old vivacity although he still had the air of someone convalescing from an illness. He was at his most ingratiating, his boyish charm taking on an appeasing modesty as if he could not bear the thought of being disliked. Immediately alerted by Harry's gravity, he asked anxiously, 'What's up?' Instead of answering, Harry told him to sit down in much the same voice as he had used to say it to Debbie that morning. Alistair sat on the sofa by the window where Harry had indicated. Without further comment, Harry picked up the typescript of Debbie's article and handed it to Alistair. 'You'd better read this,' he said simply, then he walked to the other side of the room so that Thurston could react in privacy. But he could not, in fact, take his eyes off Thurston's face. He was determined to find out how fair Priscilla Burford's account had been, and Thurston's response would tell him everything. There was, as well, a sadistic curiosity to see the effect that her description of events would have on him. The anger that Harry felt toward Thurston for being the cause of his own troubles that day sought revenge, and it was not altogether without satisfaction that he presented him with this deeply unflattering picture of himself.

Thurston's face, always inclined to be pale, went white as he read. At one point, he shut his eyes as if he could not stand any more. Then, forcing himself to carry on, he went through to the end. Priscilla had recounted, in appalling detail, his relentless pursuit of her. In her bitterness at the outcome, she had reiterated with great emphasis, all of her reluctance. *I never wanted to get involved with him . . . He wouldn't leave me alone . . . I told him again and again that I couldn't see him but he wouldn't take 'no' for an answer . . . If I refused to speak to him on the phone, he would come to the gallery and not go until I left with him.*

What she did not say, in her eagerness to disown the affair, was that she had always found him irresistible in person. The reason that he had resorted to coming to find her at the gallery was because he knew that, while she might want to finish with him in principle, she always weakened when she saw him. She did not say either, in this wretched interview, that she had had moments of sublime happiness with him, both in and out of bed. The image of himself as besotted with unrequited passion, pestering her endlessly into occasional submission, was so humiliating that it almost overshadowed the moral disrepute whose exposure would certainly ruin him. To see this piece published would be like being stripped naked and publicly horsewhipped.

Harry watched him drop the article on to the coffee table and cover his face with his hands. Then Alistair removed his handkerchief from his pocket and pressed it against his mouth, his eyes tightly shut.

'Do you want a drink?' Harry asked. Alistair nodded, unable to speak. Harry poured a large whisky and set it on the table as he sat down opposite him. For a further few seconds, Alistair remained paralysed. Then he removed the handkerchief and took a deep breath. Unable to enjoy the role of torturer any longer, Harry said firmly, 'I'm not printing it.' Alistair exhaled abruptly with intense relief. He opened his eyes then, took the whisky and drank it so quickly that it nearly gagged him. Sitting back on the sofa, he cupped the heels of his hands over his eyes, fighting off the light-headedness left by the whisky. Harry waited, morbidly fascinated by Thurston's ordeal and in no doubt at all now about the truth of Priscilla Burford's story.

At last, Alistair looked as if he might be recovering his powers of speech. Having had the terrifying threat of publication removed, he was left to feel the full personal effect of what Priscilla had said. Harry, for all his disinclination to sympathize, could see that he was desperately hurt. Debbie would be pleased, he thought ironically, at how deep a blow she had struck. Thurston leant forward, wiping his handkerchief over his face and said in a hoarse voice, 'She didn't find me that hard to take, actually.' Harry almost smiled. That it was his sexual vanity which Alistair was most anxious to salvage was an impulse which he could understand. Not permitting Alistair's suffering to weaken him, Harry said, in a tone which betrayed the day's frustration, 'Why the hell couldn't you have stayed away from her when she asked you to?'

Alistair looked as if he might well burst into tears but he recovered himself and said defensively, 'She'd just got under my skin.' And then he added pointedly, 'You know what it's like.' Harry was silenced on this point because he did know what it was like. He started on a different line, his voice still cold but less furious. 'Have you offered to give her any help? Her life is in ruins.' Alistair could reply very quickly to this, with disarming openness. 'I've tried. I wanted her to see my solicitor. Harvey Wynne has spoken to her father a few times. But she won't have anything to do with me. If we have any contact now it will be damaging for her when her divorce comes up.'

Harry nodded resignedly, knowing that this would be true. He was relieved to hear that Thurston had made such an effort. It made his own complicity feel less shoddy. 'You know,' he said slowly, 'that we can sit on this now but we can't stop it coming out in her divorce testimony. She may show your letters in Court.' This thought was more than Thurston could bear. If it had been possible to die of dread and mortification, Harry thought Alistair would have done it. Harry said more gently, 'Let's deal with that when we come to it, shall we? If she and her husband reach a settlement so that the divorce is uncontested, it may never happen. In the meantime can you call off all this talk about her?'

Alistair looked genuinely innocent. 'None of that was my idea,' he protested. 'It seemed to have a momentum of its own.'

'Well, put the word around that you want it stopped. And so will I.'

Alistair nodded. He was so chastened by Harry's willingness to protect him that he could tolerate any amount of scolding.

'Does anybody else know the full story?' Harry asked. Thurston paused. 'Her friends at the gallery, I suppose,' he said, recalling with appalled anxiety how indiscreet he had been in their presence. Harry sighed. 'Let's hope nobody asks them to give any interviews.'

Alistair, becoming more lucid, was excruciatingly aware of how much trouble he was being to his friends and colleagues, of how many people were risking their own reputations to save him. He wanted to express his gratitude to Harry but knew that saying anything explicit would only irritate him. His most eloquent thanks could be expressed in the meek acquiescence he was offering to Fitzjohn's anger. Having a strip torn off him by someone so apparently benign was almost reassuring – like being reprimanded by one of the more fair-minded prefects at school.

Now that some of the tension was gone, he was beginning to feel ill, the effects of emotional trauma and whisky making him less than sanguine about the drive he faced to Yorkshire.

'Do you think I could have some coffee?' he asked weakly. Harry stood up and went to ask the porter to have coffee and sandwiches sent up from the canteen. With the arrival of the food, their exchanges became less terse, even Harry's brusqueness beginning to give way. Shortly after six, Alistair rose to leave, still feeling shaken but looking forward to getting home to Kate who had returned to Yorkshire three days before. As Thurston reached the door, Harry said with irritable weariness, 'I think we can manage it this time Alistair, but for Christ's sake, get your life under control, would you?'

Thurston nodded submissively, and then said goodbye with such apologetic gratitude that Harry could not help but be touched.

When he had gone, Harry rang his own flat in the hope that Debbie might be there but got no reply. Then he tried her flat and was more relieved than he wished to admit to hear her voice

'It's me,' he said shyly.

'Hello you,' she answered.

'I want to see you. Can you meet me at the flat in about an hour?'

She hesitated only for a second. 'Okay,' she said.

'I'll see you then,' he promised and rang off.

* * *

'He looked like a whipped puppy when he left,' Harry said. He was lying on the sofa with his eyes closed, Debbie sitting on the floor by his side. The exertions of this hot, trying day had left him with an aching head and an unaccustomed feeling of insecurity. He reached down to touch Debbie's bare arm, enjoying the coolness of her skin. She was still quiet and watchful although he had gone to some lengths to assure her that he had made their meeting as uncomfortable for Alistair as was humanly possible.

'Do you like him?' she asked suddenly. Somewhat taken aback by this question, he said, 'Yes, I suppose so.'

'You suppose so?' she repeated, surprised. 'You're going to a lot of trouble to protect a man you're not even sure that you like.'

He sighed resignedly. She seemed to have an extraordinary capacity for making disconcerting observations.

'I *do* like him,' Harry said sulkily. In fact, he realized, it was not an issue to which he had given much thought. Thurston was a friend, not a close one, but nonetheless, a member of his own circle. It had seemed completely natural for Harry to help bail him out when he got into trouble. One did not turn one's back on someone in such a predicament. Debbie stood up and walked to the other side of the room.

'Where are you going?' he asked, opening his eyes.

'Nowhere,' she said. He sat up then, trying to shake off the heaviness in his head.

'Come over here,' he said to her when she made no move to return. She came back and sat next to him.

'Shall we get away for the weekend?' he asked, running his finger across her knee.

'Can you?' she asked doubtfully, knowing that weekends away from his wife could be difficult to arrange.

'I'll manage it,' he said.

'Okay.' She smiled at him with her old sweetness. 'If you want to.'

* * *

Although it was a private home, it was the sort of house in which one found it difficult to imagine any domestic life taking place. The whole of the downstairs at any rate had the anonymous perfection of an official residence, the paintings and the flower arrangements seeming to have been chosen to complement one another. The first floor drawing room with its festooned drapery overlooked Lower Sloane Street and the summer evening was still light enough to permit open curtains. It was a reception for a departing American diplomat, the sort of occasion which would end early and fragment into supper parties elsewhere as it dispersed.

Nigel Burkitt, the Tory backbencher whose home it was, glided past, and, spotting Fitzjohn, seized his elbow with impish delight. 'They're all queueing up to get into your lunches,' he whispered.

Harry beamed at him. 'Just a little horsetrading,' he said with an extravagant wink. Nigel smirked. 'I'll bet they're peeing themselves with excitement – the miscellaneous lot. Going to have their day.' Then he said with the malicious amusement of an excluded bystander. 'It will be fun to watch the musical chairs.'

Harry smiled. 'Wait until they get proportional representation. That's when the Monopoly game really starts.' Nigel chortled. Replacing his empty glass on a passing tray, he looked toward the door and said, 'Aah, here comes one of the players.'

Thurston was entering through the drawing room's double doors. He was alone and he paused for only a second before a voice carolled, 'Alistair!' with triumphant warmth. Thurston smiled in his dazzlingly confident way and plunged across the room. His arrival caused a murmur of excitement to reverberate around the gathering and he was quickly surrounded. Receiving the effusive attentions of a small crowd of well-wishers, he looked ecstatic, his recovery from trauma obviously complete. Having survived near-disaster, he had become on the paradoxical whim of social judgement, something of a hero. Harry watched him from a distance which made the overhearing of conversation impossible. What he saw became a choreographed mime of proffered kisses, laughter and endearments, an occasional voice rising to become audible with booming geniality.

Nigel murmured wryly, 'He came through with a little help from his friends.' Harry smiled with private possessiveness, aware of the sense in which Alistair's survival was his own personal investment. Feeling that a share in the limelight which surrounded Thurston was his due, he moved off in his direction slowly enough not to be mistaken for one of those eager acolytes who rushed forward to greet him. He approached Thurston from behind and put a hand on his shoulder. Thurston turned his head abruptly and Harry was gratified to see his face transformed from self-satisfied ebullience to humility. Turning fully round to face him deferentially, Alistair smiled at Harry with a privileged intimacy which shut out the rest of the circle which enveloped them.

Nigel standing now with Dickie Fielding, grinned and said, 'Alistair seems to think that old Fitz is where the action is.' Dickie looked mysterious. 'I think,' he said judiciously, 'that there's a bit more to it than that.'

'What do you mean?' Nigel asked with delighted avidity. Dickie smiled. 'I've heard that Fitz pulled him out of the shit in a really spectacular way.'

'Oh yes?' Nigel urged him on eagerly.

'Don't know *all* the details,' Dickie drawled with tantalizing hesitation. Nigel pulled an impatient face which made it clear that he wished to know however little information Dickie was able to offer.

'Apparently the lady in question told *her* side of the story in an interview with a *Daily News* reporter and Harry killed it stone dead,' Dickie said with pride at the dramatic impact of his bit of gossip.

'*Really?*' Nigel breathed, satisfyingly impressed. He looked back at Fitzjohn and said with awed respect, 'The old bugger. He is determined to be a kingmaker, isn't he?'

Nigel's wife floated toward Thurston with the serene condescension of a dowager duchess. He and Fitzjohn both turned to her and she presented her cheek to Alistair who kissed it with the sincere warmth which he always manifested toward women who were attentive to him. Anne Burkitt asked after Kate and Alistair replied graciously that she would be in London the following week and that the Burkitts must come to dinner while she was in town. Nigel came to join them now, sliding into their coterie beside his wife.

'Alistair was just saying,' Anne said to him, 'that we should come to dinner when Kate is down next week.'

'How nice,' Nigel enthused and beaming at both Thurston and Fitzjohn, he said, 'You're both staying on for supper here tonight, aren't you?'

Anne, too well-composed to look startled, registered only a very small note of surprise which she immediately concealed with an effusion of persuasion. She had known that Alistair had been asked to stay for their smaller dinner party after the reception but the extension of the invitation to Fitzjohn was unexpected. She would have to ask Nigel at the first possible moment what had possessed him to do that.

* * *

Fortunately, Debbie was at home in her flat when the telephone call came. The voice at the other end was so hesitant that at first it was unrecognizable.

'Who is this?' she asked.

'It's Priscilla.'

'Oh, Priscilla! How are you?' There was a pause. Then Priscilla said, 'I wondered if you knew yet when your article was going to come out.'

Wanting to equivocate out of embarrassment, she had to force herself to admit the truth. 'I'm afraid I'm having some trouble with it. Harry is a friend of Thurston's and he doesn't want to use it.'

There was no sound from the telephone at all and Debbie said, 'Priscilla, are you there?'

'Yes,' Priscilla answered quickly and Debbie could hear that she was crying.

'What's wrong, Priscilla. What's happened?'

It took a few seconds for the answer to come. 'Julian is saying,' she began, trying to control her voice, 'that he's going to fight for custody of the children.'

'Oh, my God,' Debbie said quietly.

'My solicitor says,' Priscilla carried on, 'that the Courts are very sympathetic these days to men wanting custody. He says . . . ' she stopped for a second. 'He says that all the publicity will prejudice things against me . . . ' Her voice trailed off. It was unbearable to listen to her desperation. Debbie realized that waiting for this article to appear must have been like a lifeline.

'Look,' Debbie said. 'If Harry won't have it in the *Daily News*, I may be able to sell it somewhere else.'

'Do you think you could?' Priscilla asked, her voice dreadfully hopeful.

'You know the English papers.' Debbie wanted to involve her in the plans as a kind of therapy for her despair. 'Which one would be most likely to take it?'

'I'd have thought any of the tabloids,' Priscilla said somewhat ruefully, but then her voice picked up some of its old competence as she reflected. 'The *Mirror* would be very keen to sink a Tory minister.'

'Right,' Debbie said decisively. 'I'll try them.'

'Will Harry be angry?' Priscilla felt obliged to ask, suspecting in fact that Debbie had Fitzjohn so firmly twisted around her finger that there could be little danger to their relationship.

'Don't worry about that,' Debbie's confident voice came back. 'I'll deal with Harry.'

'Okay,' Priscilla said, her relief almost palpable.

'I'll ring you to tell you what's happening. And the *Mirror* may ring you as well.'

'Thanks very much, Debbie,' Priscilla replied warmly.

'That's okay. Don't worry. I'll be in touch.'

After she had rung off, she telephoned the *Mirror* and asked to speak to the Features Editor. It was an assistant to the Features Editor who answered.

'I want to know whether you'd be interested in an interview with Priscilla Burford.'

'Who?' the assistant said tersely.

'Priscilla Burford – the woman Alistair Thurston had an affair with.'

'She isn't giving any interviews, love. We've tried,' he said dismissively.

'I *have* done an interview with her. She's given me the whole story of her relationship with Thurston. I'm offering to sell it to you.' Debbie's voice was taking on the painstaking exasperation which she often found necessary in dealing with Fleet Street editors.

'You've done an interview with her?' He sounded frankly sceptical. 'Who are you?'

'I'm Debbie Ackerman. I'm a freelance journalist and I've known Priscilla for a long time. That's why she was willing to talk to me.' Her clarity was beginning to persuade him. He asked more respectfully, 'When was the interview done?'

'Two weeks ago.'

'Have you ever done anything for us?'

'No, but I've written for the *Daily News* and the *Mail*.'

'Hang on a minute love, would you?'

She waited, knowing that he was now taking her seriously. When he came back, his voice was agreeable and friendly. 'Could you bring it in and let us see it?' he said. Yes, she could, she replied and they arranged for her to come straight in.

★ ★ ★

The whole floor was open-plan with sections partitioned off by dividing screens, the top half of which were frosted glass. Debbie was told to sit down in front of a desk, by a harassed looking woman who needed Debbie's name repeated three times before she took it in. After ten minutes, a middle-aged man in his shirtsleeves appeared around the corner of the dividing partition. 'Hi,' he said. 'Are you Debbie Ackerman?' It was the same voice she had heard on the telephone and she nodded.

'Right then.' Flinging himself down into the chair behind the desk, he said with cheerful exuberance, 'Let's see this interview.'

She pulled the neatly folded typescript out of her canvas bag and watched him read it, racing through it quickly as editors always did. When he had finished, he whistled and drummed his fingers on the desk.

'I've also got,' Debbie said with cool, professional composure, 'copies of some of the letters she mentions.'

'Have you?' he asked, looking up intently. Then he stood up with her typescript in his hand. 'Just hang on a minute.' He gave her a cheerful wink. 'I'll be right back.'

It was almost a quarter of an hour before he returned and she knew that this was a good sign. He was probably having other people read it. When he reappeared, he was openly friendly and solicitous.

'Right,' he said, sitting on his desk. 'We're going to need to ring her to get confirmation that the interview is genuine and arrange for a photograph.'

Debbie reached into her bag once more and produced her address book. She gave them the Hertfordshire number where they could contact Priscilla.

'Great,' he said as he took it from her. 'Have you got those letters with you?'

'I'll give you the letters,' Debbie said with a smile, 'when we agree the price.'

He grinned at her. 'What figure did you have in mind?'

'Make me an offer.'

'I'll have to have a word with the governor.'

'You do that.'

He grinned again and went off. He was gone another ten minutes.

'The man says five thousand,' he said, perching on a corner of the desk. She looked at him carefully knowing that this was a gambit. 'Eight,' she said. He pulled a warning face and shook his head 'Six and not a penny more.'

She shrugged. 'Okay,' she said standing up. 'As long as I get a by-line.'

'Sure,' he agreed cheerfully.

She gave him the photocopied letters then and watched his face light up as he read them.

When she came out onto Holborn, it was starting to rain. The summer seemed to have expired in the last few days into the kind of cool overcast which often settled onto an English August. She walked to Fleet Street and carried on down the length of the Strand, invigorated by the coolness of the air. By the time she reached Trafalgar Square, she was wet through. She went into the National Gallery and walked slowly through the early Italian rooms allowing their melancholy serenity to dominate her state of mind. Wandering along her favourite path she found herself in front of Holbein's 'The Ambassadors'. She gazed for a while at those two triumphantly confident representatives of the Renaissance with their own mortality hidden like a secret joke in the painting. Then she left the Gallery and went to book her trip to Florence.